The Murderous Urges of Ordinary Women

The Murderous Urges of Ordinary Women

by Lois Meltzer

The characters and events in this book are fictitious. Any similarity to any persons living or dead is coincidental and not intended by the author.

Published by Certain Age Press, Seattle, Washington
www.certainagepress.com

Printed in the USA

ISBN: 9780615160894

LCCN 2007906530

Cataloging-In-Publication Data

Meltzer, Lois.
The murderous urges of ordinary women / by Lois Meltzer.
p. ; cm.
ISBN: 978-0-615-16089-4

1. Middle-aged women--Fiction. 2. Book clubs (Discussion groups) --Fiction. 3. Revenge--Fiction. 4. Humorous fiction. I. Title.

PS3613.E4659 M87 2007
813/.6

2007906530

Book design by CompassRose.com
Cover design by Vedic Designs

To Judith and Celia,
"The Dollinks"

Prologue

The Beginning

See, ever since the four of us—me and Janet, Ellie and Carole—met in the book group, we'd had a regular dinner date the third Wednesday of the month. It used to be we'd go ethnic and cheap. But lately, someone always seemed to say "nothing too spicy," so we'd wind up at a salad bar, or a vegan joint where everything tasted like stewed styrofoam.

However on the night I'm talking about, the night it all started, we found ourselves instead at this tourist trap called Cap'n Ahab's. You know the kind of place—the doorknobs are miniature anchors, the restroom signs say "Gulls" and "Buoys," and the first thing you see when you walk in is a tank full of doomed lobsters. Not exactly our usual cup of herbal tea. So maybe it was Fate that Carole had that coupon which was about to expire, and she couldn't stand to see go to waste. Because if we'd gone somewhere else, the whole business with the cellphone might never have happened, and our lives might have turned out differently.

Things went wrong right from the beginning.

Only valet parking was available, which practically ruined Carole's meal before she even stepped through the door.

Then the Maitre d' ignored us, which infuriated Ellie, who is easily infuriated, for a Buddhist.

"What I really hate about getting older," she growled, "is

that all of a sudden it's as if I've become invisible."

Now while *invisible* isn't the word that immediately springs to mind to describe Eleanor Van Deuvel—six feet tall, two hundred fifty pounds, with a cloud of bright orange hair like a child's drawing of a sunset—we knew what she meant: once you arrive at what the French gallantly call a "certain age" (and Americans ungallantly refer to as "being past your pull date"), nobody seems to notice you anymore. And until it happens, you didn't realize you'd been accustomed most of your adult life to being noticed, or at least to portions of you being noticed: your hair, your legs, your breasts, your butt. Not that you necessarily welcomed the attention at the time.

Then they seated us at a cramped table next to the kitchen, which put me in a resentful frame of mind.

"Why do they always stick women our age in the back where no one can see us," I wondered out loud, "as if we clashed with the nautical décor?"

We laughed, but it made us angry: our invisibility, our irrelevance.

And that wasn't all that made us angry. This is what you must understand.

More and more, the routine irritations of modern life—stuff that merely used to annoy us—now seemed to fill us with this murderous, impotent rage:

People who hog two spaces in the parking lot. People who force you to listen in on their boring cellphone conversations. People who don't clean up after their dogs. Young people whose every other word is *fuckthisfuckthatfuckingwhatthefuck*. Developers who tear up farmland to build ugly mini-mansions one right on top of the other. The people who buy them. Trophy wives. The decline of civilization.

Maybe it's a menopause thing.

"Why is it that restaurants are always too hot or too cold?" Ellie shivered, drawing her vintage shawl around her bare shoulders.

We glanced up. Sure enough, our table was located directly beneath a belching air vent. It figured.

"I'm absolutely freezing," Janet said.

"Intolerable," Carole said.

The others looked at me.

Over the years, somehow it had become my job to handle any potentially unpleasant encounters with restaurant personnel. "You're a lawyer, Sandi," Carole would point out. "You enjoy confrontation." Not true. I hate confrontation. I'd quit my profession in a heartbeat and write small volumes of poems instead, if only someone would pay me $100,000 a year to do it.

I tracked down the waiter, a hulking person whose nametag declared him to be "Chad."

"You might have said something before I went and poured the water." He raised his Cap'n Ahab eye-patch so he could scowl at me full in the face.

"We didn't *notice* the vent before you poured the water."

Grumbling all the way, he slammed down the glasses and silverware on our new improved table and disappeared, apparently for good.

"Well there goes his tip," Carole muttered. "What an attitude."

"No!"

Janet struck the air with her tiny fists, surprisingly forceful for such a bird-like woman.

"He's entitled to an attitude." She looked around, as if daring us to disagree. "He barely makes minimum wage, and has to wear an eye-patch and a shirt with scenes from 'The Little Mermaid.'"

Count on Janet to take the waiter's side. She is a truly good person who always sympathizes with the underdog, even such an unpromising specimen of the breed as Chad.

I love Janet dearly, but there are times she can make you feel a little morally bankrupt.

So with one thing and another, I was already in a foul mood by the time *he* sat down at the next table. He was a Type: about 40, deeply tanned, seriously blow-dried, overbearing voice, Master of the Universe swagger. Another of the things we hated: guys like him.

Right off, he started in with the cellphone: *Offer them a million five, and if they say no, fuck 'em.*

Each of us glared at him separately. The four of us glared together. We loudly lamented the rude intrusion of private conversations into public space. All wasted. He just kept on going, informing the world at large of his itinerary:

"...then on Thursday I fly to Mazatlan for a meeting, and on Saturday I'm in Atlanta for a trade conference..."

And when Ellie tapped him on the shoulder and said, "Could you please keep it down?" he replied, "Could you please (obscene gesture)?"

"So long. Gotta take a piss," he suddenly announced to the person on the other end of the line, (t*hanks for sharing, mister*), and began heading toward the facilities near the entrance. In his haste to relieve himself, he'd left his phone behind—an expensive all-over-the-world model, I noticed. Great, I thought, he can be an asshole *from* anywhere on the planet *to* anywhere on the planet.

It seemed so *wrong*; so fundamentally *wrong*.

Moved by some force larger than myself, I rose from my seat.

I swiped the phone.

I meandered over to the lobster tank.

I tossed the phone in.

Splash!!

And here's the thing: Yes, somebody might have seen, but the thing is, nobody *noticed*.

Later, as I watched The Dealmaker searching frantically among the crumpled napkins, scanning every table but ours for the responsible party, a realization dawned—an intimation of an enormous and unsuspected possibility, like a seductive whisper from some fierce, ancient female spirit, some Ur-Crone out of the collective unconscious:

Women our age are invisible.

Women our age are not taken seriously.

Women our age might be able to get away with...anything. Absolutely anything.

Melissa Crane shut off the tape recorder.

"So that's what gave you all the idea for the website and the rest, that epiphany there in Cap'n Ahab's. What a name. Like —'Call me Fishmeal.'"

I couldn't help feeling well-disposed toward a young person who used the word "epiphany," even though she wore an eyebrow ring and had mysterious Japanese characters covering her left bicep.

"It means 'Satori,'" she'd said when she saw me staring. "It's from my Eastern religion phase. Enlightenment and all that shit. I am so past it now."

Melissa Crane didn't look old enough to have had an Eastern religion phase, much less to have a Ph.D. and be writing a book on post-feminist feminism. But then, that's one of the disconcerting things about middle-age, suddenly noticing all these 12-year-olds behind the wheel, and the physicians barely out of puberty.

"The website? Oh no, that came much later," I said, "after the whole business with Lex Viper."

"Viper? The action star? The one who…"

"Yes, that was our doing, though he never realized it, of course."

"Cool," she raised her fist. "You ROCK."

She turned the recorder back on, and motioned me to continue.

"But it didn't start with anything big or dramatic," I reminisced. "It began with what you might call mischief…"

"Mischief? I'd call it a little more than mischief…"

"Not in the beginning," I said. "We weren't really all that different from other women our age in the beginning. Fifty is a time for new enthusiasms; for taking adult education courses on how to play the autoharp or write mystery novels or speak Portuguese. Our new hobby was …

…Discover your Inner Vigilante 101: Always had a secret yen to be a super-hero, but didn't know how to get started? This class will acquaint you with the basics. Through guided imagery and fun non-threatening group exercises, you will learn to identify your own personal style. Are you a Mighty Mouse? A Wonder Woman? A Ninja Princess? Field trip to mystery location where we practice skills learned in class, including how to let air out of tires using nothing but a Number Two pencil!

"But as I said, it started with small things, with each of us seeing an opportunity and impulsively seizing it. Only later did it become something more ambitious, more organized, more…vengeful, I suppose…

"For me, it started with that cellphone.

"For Ellie it began with a nasty piece of work who stole Ellie's parking space at Prime Foods one Saturday afternoon. Big mistake."

Book One

Ellie

Chapter One

Ellie Goes to Market

Ellie drove around the lot once, twice, three times. No luck. She breathed deeply, centering herself. She would *not* hurl curses at the Suburban straddling two spots. She would *not* honk her horn at the pickup squeezing itself into a "compact only" space. She would *not* sound off at those two nitwits setting up little Courtney's/Sean's play dates instead of promptly loading their packages into their global-warming SUVs. No. Anger is a cold wind that blows out the lamp of the spirit. That's what Shanti Goldfarb, her meditation teacher, said.

She would resort instead to a desperate last-ditch maneuver—stalking some shopper from the store exit and lying in wait, though Ellie suspected this might be a breach of an unspoken rule of parking etiquette. But what else could she do? It was already half past four, and Ramon would be over at eight expecting his raw oysters. As it was, she'd barely have time to rush home, cook dinner, clean, set the table, shower, dress in—yes, the French maid's costume tonight—put on makeup, light the scented candles...

She soon spotted her quarry, a young man lightly loaded, and trailed him to a green Volkswagen not far from the entrance. Perfect. Couldn't be better. Maybe Shanti was right. When you calm down and get in tune with the Universe, the Universe really does get in tune with you.

Ellie backed up. The Volkswagen pulled out. Then—catastrophe! Before she could even shift into drive, a big silver-blue Mercedes roared into the vacant space, *Ellie's* vacant space, as if it were *entitled* by divine decree from the God of Really Expensive Cars.

Ellie seethed as she watched the driver emerge, a woman in her thirties, thin and blonde, wearing Spandex cycling shorts and a cropped top that showed off her rippled midriff—the kind of woman who, even under the best of circumstances, Ellie had to make a deep spiritual effort not to hate at first sight.

These were not the best of circumstances.

"Stupid asshole!" Ellie screamed. "That was my space."

The woman shrugged, turned away from Ellie, and shouted into the interior of the glossy machine: "Meredith honey, hurry up. Mommy's got ten people coming for dinner tonight."

A child materialized from the passenger side, the child pert and blond like her mother, and with the self-satisfied look of a spoiled brat who'd never been denied anything. This Meredith reminded Ellie of Betty Sue McCluskey, Queen of Bunk Three at Camp Winnemucca, who had nicknamed Ellie "Lardbutt," and made Ellie's long-ago eighth summer Hell on Earth.

"Asshole!" Ellie screamed again, leaping out of the car.

The little girl stared at Ellie, and Ellie was conscious of what she must look like, furious as she was—tomato red cheeks, concentric chins vibrating like turkey wattles.

"That fat lady called you a bad name," Meredith lisped. "That wasn't very nice."

The mother, ever alert to the possibility of a teachable

moment, slowly surveyed Ellie's mass, and whispered loud enough so Ellie could hear:

"Never mind. Some people are like that. It's because they've got Low Self-Esteem."

Ellie felt the familiar pounding in her temples. She closed her eyes and breathed deeply. No use. She opened her eyes. Mother and child had gotten to her, hit a nerve which Ellie had thought was numb and dead by now. After all, hadn't she spent years in therapy with Dr. Burns learning to accept herself as she was—not fat, but big...voluptuous, Rubenesque. And, as Janet pointed out, largeness itself is a culturally relative concept. In Tonga, for instance, Ellie would've been considered downright bony.

Unfortunately Ellie didn't live in Tonga, or in any of the other hot and humid places where, according to Janet, Big is Sexy. So Ellie had endured the subtle contempt visited on the publicly oversized here in the temperate zone. It had taken a long time and a fortune in psychiatrist's fees, but finally, at age 47, Ellie managed to feel good about herself 95% of the time. She had many friends. She had her work as a photographer. And there were men, like Ramon, who actually preferred a full-figured woman.

But every once in a while, there would be a casual remark from some scrawny bitch in a Mercedes or her spawn, and it would come flooding back—all the humiliations of a lifetime of Blimp, Tubby, Wide-load, Whale, Elephant—and Ellie would feel the rage rise within her, and she'd want to do terrible things.

She didn't have time for rage, not now, with raw oysters to buy, plus the ingredients for leek and fennel soup. She closed her eyes again, slowed down the motions of her mind the way Shanti had taught her, and focused on a single word: Shalom. (Shanti's meditation techniques combined the best of Eastern and Western spiritual traditions). And more slowly: *sha-a-a-lo-o-ohm.* She began to lose herself in the benign emptiness of the whatever-you-choose-to-call-the-Higher-Power...then re-membered she had no time for benign emptiness. Or Higher Powers. Gritting her teeth, she circled the lot once more, fi-nally scoring a semi-legal spot way off on the periphery; then running the two blocks to the entrance huffing, puffing, worst of all, perspiring. Never again, she swore, would she make the mistake of shopping at Prime Foods on a Saturday after-noon.

The Prime, as everyone called it, was the hottest new gro-cery store/food marketing concept in the entire city, and for good reason. The produce displays alone were almost worth the drive: the careful contrasts of color, shape and texture; the tidy pyramids of unblemished limes and oranges; the pale nubby daikon set against the flawless eggplant...maybe a little too flawless for Ellie's personal taste. Ellie believed there was no true beauty without some slight imperfection, and she tried to convey that in her photographs, which often focused on rust and decay. But if you weren't talking about True Beauty, if you were talking about nicely arranged fruits and vegetables, Prime Foods was hard to beat.

It wasn't the presentation alone, however, that made Prime Foods so special. You could sip your morning cappuccino in one of the leather armchairs by the fireplace or eat your pa-nini sandwich at a table in the flagstone-paved garden, with its hanging baskets of bright flowers. In short, there was no more pleasant place to shop on a weekday morning than Prime Foods.

But on the weekends, when the suburban mothers descended, brats in tow, Ellie ordinarily avoided the place like poison.

She wished sometimes that she could appreciate children more. Certainly they were beautiful to look at with their porcelain complexions and neat miniature limbs. It was everything else about them she disliked: their annoying, high-pitched voices; their abrupt, unpredictable movements; the way they disturbed your energy field like a gunshot on a lazy summer afternoon. And people brought them everywhere now. Even last week, at that lecture on Transcendental Humming, somebody's out-of-control five-year-old had been sprinting up and down the aisles of the church. What was the mother thinking? Ellie had turned to the solemn older Korean woman in the next seat and said she felt sorry for the child, being dragged along to something like this. But really, she hadn't felt sorry for the child at all. The person she'd felt sorry for was herself.

Now she'd have to endure a half-hour in a crush of them, just to get the dozen raw oysters she'd promised Ramon. Raw oysters wasn't exactly the kind of thing she could pick up at her local Safeway, where it was only last month they'd finally added cilantro to the parsley lineup.

She liked Ramon all right, but she was beginning to wonder, was he really worth the bother? Leaving aside his lack of gainful employment, his vague immigration status and his occasional lapses in grooming, now there was his ever-increasing need for these hard-to-find supposed aphrodisiacs. What next? Powdered rhinoceros horn?

She'd been dating Ramon for a year, a near-record for Ellie, especially for someone she'd found on the internet. "Small man wants big beautiful woman for fun and games, maybe more," his profile had read, which Ellie translated as: "Commitment-phobic midget seeks desperate kinky fat gal."

He'd been a pleasant surprise when they finally met at Starbucks. Ramon was only six inches shorter than she was, and good-looking, like something sleek and furry but not especially nice—a ferret, maybe. Then, first thing, he'd handed her a single wilted orange rose he must have picked up from a florist's discard pile. The French call this flower the Thigh of an Aroused Nymph, he'd told her, instantly establishing his credentials as a romantic, if not as a botanist.

They hadn't had sex until their fourth date, that's how big a romantic Ramon was. He said he liked to woo a woman first, it was his Latin way. This wooing process didn't involve the actual expenditure of money, of course. On date two they'd walked on the beach at sunset. On date three they'd watched boats in the harbor. On date four, after a day of window-shopping downtown, he'd asked her if she'd like to fulfill one of his secret fantasies. She said what she usually said when men asked her this, which is, "Sure, provided it doesn't involve the cat-o-nine-tails." So Ramon put on a wig and a muumuu he'd concealed in his backpack, and she snuck him into the Women's Lounge at Nordstrom, where they'd had sex in the handicapped stall. Decent sex, given the location, but Ellie couldn't really relax and enjoy it. What if some woman in a wheelchair needed to use the toilet? Ellie would feel terrible. Still it had been wild, and he couldn't get enough of her back then. Now, barely a year later, it had come to this: costumes, supplements, the occasional pornographic movie, the better part of a Saturday afternoon wasted at Prime Foods, buying oysters.

She braced herself and activated the sliding glass door.

Inside it was as bad as she'd feared. You could hardly see the exquisite groceries for the shoppers clogging the narrow aisles, not to mention the little "customers-in-training" ramming their tiny pink plastic carts into the shins of the slower moving oldsters.

Ever so carefully she inched through the produce department, maneuvering her bulk so she wouldn't accidentally dislodge a crate of cantaloupes or tumble a lime pyramid in her backwash. The potential for such mortification was always there, Ellie knew, for the plus-sized. Only a week ago she had nearly toppled a wine rack at the Safeway when Ellie had been forced to stop short to avoid a collision with a Pepsi deliveryman.

And now little Meredith and the awful woman from the Mercedes were blocking the path, the woman demanding that a harried clerk personally escort her to the lemongrass. She was having ten people to dinner, the woman announced. She was making her famous Brazilian-Thai chicken with fragrant rice. The clerk waved in the direction of the Asian exotics. I already looked there, the woman insisted. I need you to come over and show me.

"Excuse me," Ellie said, "Can I get through?"

"Just a minute." The woman handed the clerk a can.

"This coconut milk is from the Philippines. I needed the Thai coconut milk."

"Excuse me," Ellie said again, with more of an edge to her

voice. "If you could just move to the side…"

The woman turned, and once again surveyed Ellie's mass.

"There's plenty of room," she drawled. "I left plenty of room."

"For a normal size person," little Meredith smirked and pushed at Ellie's cart, causing Ellie to lurch backwards, lose her balance and knock over three jars of gourmet salad dressing. "Cleanup on aisle one," the clerk shouted, as the other shoppers stared at red-faced Ellie and at the gelatinous ooze spreading near her feet.

Meredith giggled (the identical heartless giggle of Betty Sue McCluskey), and said to her mother, in a voice like sugar, or rather sugar-substitute:

"It's because she's got such a big butt, right Mommy? Because she has no self-control, right Mommy?"

And so it got passed on from generation to generation, Ellie thought, and felt the ominous pounding in her head, the firecrackers behind her eyes, the urge to lash out, to roar, to grab mother and daughter behind their elegant necks and shove their smug faces over and over into that flat of blueberries over there. Ellie breathed deeply, remembering that it was just such urges that had driven her to Shanti Goldfarb in the first place. Or rather it was one particular urge that had resulted in Ellie breaking a beer bottle over the head of an obnoxious drunk at a party who had announced that he would rather fuck a pregnant hippopotamus than Ellie (not that Ellie was offering). That's when Ellie realized she might have a problem—when the police had been called and the drunk had to be talked out of pressing charges.

Violence isn't the answer, Shanti had said. Violence is never the answer. There are better ways to express your feelings than violence.

Ellie closed her eyes, chanted sha-a-lohm. By the time she'd finished, the woman had moved on and Ellie was calm enough to continue with her shopping, passing efficiently through the dense aisles. Oysters, fennel, leeks, potatoes, baguette, salad, and a few earth-friendly cleaning supplies she figured she might as well pick up as long as she was here anyway.

She spotted the woman again at the checkout stand—the 12 items or less, even though Ellie counted a good 20 items in the woman's cart. Ellie parked her own cart just behind, and that's how she happened to hear the woman instructing the cashier to put all the ingredients for the famous Brazilian-Thai chicken into one bag, with the recipe on top, so the woman wouldn't have to assemble things when she got home. Little Meredith meanwhile pulled at her mother's arm, whining, "I need to go to the bathroom really bad."

"Well hurry," the woman said. "I've got ten people coming to dinner."

Ellie paid for her groceries and decided to take a quick trip to the Ladies herself before the long drive home. And then the Universe intervened again for Ellie, because the woman's loaded cart was parked outside the restroom door, and the woman's voice could be heard from inside yelling, "How long does it take you to do a number one, for Chrissake?"

The substitution only took a second—Ellie's bag of cleaning supplies for the bag full of all the ingredients for Brazilian-Thai chicken. Ellie placed the recipe on the top of the substituted bag, noticing, with satisfaction, that it was one of those stern, unforgiving recipes that discourage deviation. "If you can't find the fresh chilies you can use the canned, but it just won't taste the same...If you don't make your own fish stock you can substitute clam juice, but the flavor will be a lot less intense."

She laughed and shook her bountiful hips. Ramon loved her hips, said they reminded him of great mounds of fluffy mashed potatoes. Sometimes he would pour warm gravy on them and murmur deep yum-yums into her belly. Yes, Ramon could be fun. Maybe she would make Brazilian-Thai chicken for ten tonight and let him take home the leftovers. He was always starving.

Shanti was right. Violence was not the answer. There were better ways for Ellie to express her feelings than violence. So on the way back to her own car, the very long way back, she rammed her shopping cart deep, deep into the door of a certain silver-blue Mercedes for good measure.

Emergency Mock Brazilian Thai Chicken (without the basil, lemon grass, coconut milk, jasmine rice, tomatoes or chicken)

Ingredients:

- Fried onion rings
- Box Ritz Barbecue flavor crackers
- Can Campbell's chicken soup with wild rice and vegetables (you can substitute the store brand, but it just won't taste the same).

Combine crackers and soup in casserole dish. Top with onions. Bake at 350 degrees until warmed through. Make sure guests are well-pickled before serving.

"Men are scum," Melissa Crane said. She had dyed her short spiky hair a deep purple since we last met. It suited her.

She was referring, I supposed, to Ethan, the actor with major intimacy issues who had recently dumped her, and who I'd heard much too much about already.

"Some men may be scum all of the time," I objected. "And maybe all men are scum some of the time. But all men aren't scum all of the time." With age comes moderation. With raising a perfectly nice son, as I have, comes even more moderation.

"Well," she acknowledged, "maybe just all actors are scum."

She turned on the recorder.

"Speaking of scummy actors, can we talk about Lex Viper today? I'm dying to know how you pulled it off."

"Ah yes, The Viper. It was simple really," I said, "once we got the basic idea and put the wheels in motion. It all began at another of our Wednesday night dinners, this time at a little place called the 'Seventh Chakra' over in the University District…"

Chapter Two

Girls Night Out at the Movies

"Dull, grey, flat, and stale," Janet winced at her plate of garbanzo-loaf with braised tofu.

"It's not that bad," Ellie said, "except for the texture."

The "Seventh Chakra" had been Ellie's pick, recommended by an elderly artist friend who'd praised its "good vibrations." The place appeared to be run by some kind of cult which didn't believe either in using salt or pre-soaking legumes. What they did believe in, according to the brochures scattered around the tables, was that World Peace begins with personal transformation.

"I think I just broke a tooth on a lentil," Carole said.

Janet shook her head.

"No, I wasn't talking about the food. I was describing the state I'm in. How dull, flat, stale and unprofitable seem to me all the uses of the world. Or something like that. It's from *Hamlet*, which I'm being forced to teach this quarter, God help me."

Janet taught in the English department at the local Community College, a real challenge, it seemed, when the course description didn't include the term "remedial."

"It isn't easy getting students to engage with the written word," Janet sighed. "Especially the 400-year-old written word."

"We're entering another dark age," Carole agreed, "when the only people who read for pleasure will be a few monks someplace in Bavaria. Everybody else will be watching Die Hard 127.

"Print just can't compete with the more visceral pleasures of movie-watching," Carole continued, quoting from an article she'd pulled out of the enormous tapestry purse where she kept her clippings of current interest. "Listen to this: *'What does a movie do? A movie distills reality into image, transforms fantasy into fact, offers a vision of deep communal pleasure and at the same time, of utter atomized disaffection—at once collective and radically alone—"*

Which explains, I guess, why my son Alexander and his buddies will cheerfully fork over nine bucks to watch two hours of cars getting exploded.

This was another of our favorite complaints about American culture—that the average movie was made *by* someone with the mentality of a 16-year-old boy *for* someone with the mentality of a 16-year-old boy. If only movies could be made *by* people with the mentality of a 50-year-old woman *for* people with the mentality of a 50-year-old woman instead.

Movies would be much shorter, for one thing. Short enough so you wouldn't need to take a break in the middle, stumbling over everyone's legs and muttering "excuse me, excuse me." What few sex scenes there were would also be shorter and more true to life. People would wear flannel pajamas and get arch cramps. There would be a lot less moaning and a lot more snoring.

During every car chase a woman would be sitting in the passenger seat screaming, "Slow down you idiot, you'll get a ticket!" And there would be a warning in subtitles: *Don't you even dare think about trying this yourself at home.* Nothing would get blown up except balloons.

It would never happen, of course. We knew that. Was this because 50-year-old women can't offer a satisfying vision of communal pleasure and at the same time utter atomized disaffection in the way, say, 16-year-old boys can? Hardly.

No—it's because movies and the people who make them are the essence of what's cool. Or hot. And we middle-aged women, we're the essence of what…isn't.

And this gave us an idea…

We were only a dozen that first time…the four of us and a few of our friends. And the movie we chose was by no means the worst of its kind to come out that year, or even that month. The reviewers had described it as "action packed," noting its "non-stop action," its "action every minute," and also that there was "action from first scene to last;" the action in question consisting of a) people getting shot and b) stuff getting incinerated.

We picked *Death by Vengeance*, not for its content, but because it starred the detestable Lex Viper, adored by his fans for his serious pecs and abs, his self-regarding arrogance, and for a private life nearly as action-packed as his movies (the action in that arena consisting mainly of a) busting up hotel rooms and b) checking himself into rehab).

But even more offensive than Viper himself, was Roger "R.R." Ross, the producer of the mega-flicks. This is the same Roger Ross who had crashed and burned ten years earlier after a series of expensive flops featuring aging stars on the cusp of has-been-hood. The Viper had revived Ross' career, and in gratitude, Ross now attempted to look and act as much like his star as was possible for a short, paunchy 48-year-old man who, until he shaved his head, had been trying to kick a $500-a-month Rogaine habit. R.R. pierced both ears. He danced all night with underage girls at hip clubs. He tooted cocaine in the men's room. Viper had brought out Ross' inner bad boy, Ross told the press, and he'd never felt better in his life.

More like his inner jerk. Which is why if we were going to start out by ruining anybody, we figured it might as well be Roger Ross. He not only made terrible movies, but his lifestyle set a bad, if slightly pathetic, example for other men his age.

So we were first in line for the first showing of *Death by Vengeance* on its opening weekend in our city.

"Twelve Senior Citizen discounts," Carole announced, whipping out her AARP membership card.

"Twelve adults," I hastily corrected.

The slack-jawed boy behind me tapped my shoulder.

"I think you want, like, that line over there," he said, "for, like, the Meryl Streep thing."

I turned around so he could see the "Lex Viper Rules" T-shirt, the one with the serpent coiled around the assault rifle.

"You gotta be shitting me," his jaw grew even slacker, as a murmur went through the crowd of dateless guys under 25.

Then the 12 of us turned around, so the crowd could get a better look. We all wore "Viper Rules" T-shirts, some with the serpent coiled around the assault rifle, some with the serpent coiled around a handgun, some with no serpent at all, just Viper's hard-eyed, pouty-lipped face.

The line behind us was suddenly quiet as all these guys without dates began wondering whether that was why they *were* guys without dates: because they were so clueless that they didn't even realize that somehow, overnight, Lex Viper had become totally uncool, which is to say totally unhot. This happened, they knew. The uncoolness probably would have started in L.A. or New York, just like the coolness had, and only gradually would have reached our provincial city. Why hadn't they been told? It made them angry. They were going to go right home and spread the news over the internet to other clueless, dateless guys in places like Atlanta and Des Moines.

By the time the feature presentation started, we had the theatre practically to ourselves. Carole complained to the manager about the sound level, which was hurting our ears. We left after 15 minutes. We bought no popcorn.

While *Death by Vengeance* opened strong in New York and L.A., the box office in the rest of the country was almost nonexistent, causing speculation that maybe this was the beginning of the end for Viper; that by tomorrow he would be yesterday's star. Some of the more thoughtful critics even wondered if this was a sign of some larger trend, where the uncoolness, or unhotness, of a formerly cool, or hot, thing would begin, not on the coasts, as before, but in places like Cleveland or Albuquerque. This they attributed to the information revolution and the resulting democratization of taste.

We knew better.

"Never doubt," Carole said, quoting Margaret Mead, "that

a small group of thoughtful, committed citizens can change the world. Indeed, nothing else ever has."

She pulled another clipping from her purse. This one concerned a youth-oriented clothing line which recruited high school trend-setters to advise it on the Next Big Thing. Who are these trendsetters, the article asked? No, not necessarily the best-looking or most popular kids, though popularity and good looks didn't hurt. These lucky few just had that mysterious thing—let's call it style—and where they went, everybody else followed.

"So," Janet asked, "who cares where they go?"

"So," Carole replied, "The opposite is also true—there are people who have that mysterious thing—let's call it dorkiness, for want of a better word—and where they go, everybody else runs away. Imagine what could be accomplished if that thing—that dork-quality—could be harnessed for the benefit of humankind..."

I resented the implication.

"Are you saying you detect this thing, this dork-quality, in *us*?"

"Of course not. I'm saying we have something even better. I've said it before—as older women we have the power, merely by liking something, to make it instantly undesirable to everybody else. Think about it. The cars we drive. The TV shows we watch. The restaurants we patronize. Even our spiritual longings. Forget Nietzsche. God was *really* dead as soon as middle-aged women took him up."

We knew what she meant. (Except maybe for the Nietzsche part).

"There she goes again. What does Nietzsche have to do

with anything?" Ellie snapped.

We all respect Carole's intellect, but when she casually refers to Nietzsche or Jungian archetypes or the *zeitgeist*, the way she does, it can make the people around her feel vaguely put down, even though that isn't her intention. It's just how her mind is furnished. It's probably true, what she told me once, that she would have fit in better someplace like Paris.

"I said *forget* Nietzsche," Carole snapped back. "The point is, look what we did to Lex Viper, and that was only 12 of us in one city."

Yes, The Viper's fall had been swift and precipitous, another of those Hollywood object lessons in the perils of hubris and of letting your pecs and abs go soft. After the spectacular failure of *Death by Vengeance,* which barely earned back Viper's $10 million salary, he was reduced to starring in a combination war movie/teen laughfest called *Flatulence Now*, where his performance gave new meaning to that old theatrical adage: dying is easy; comedy is hard.

After that, there was the odd guest spot on the better cop series; then rehab again; then salvation; then his own call-in show on the Jesus is Lord network, where he specializes in reformed sinners in general and professional athletes in particular. He quotes from the Book of Revelation a lot, especially the parts where people get killed and stuff gets incinerated.

As for Roger "R.R." Ross, he soon announced his retirement from film-making, in favor of spending more time with his family, which by then consisted of a schnauzer and two goldfish, his fourth wife having left him over a couple of starlets whom she discovered in Ross' bed one afternoon, the wife having returned home early from a day at the spa after suffering an allergic reaction to an algae-based body wrap.

"It's a power we have, and like any power, it must be used sparingly and only for good," Carole said.

Janet smiled.

"Do you think if aging women everywhere came out in favor of war and other forms of mindless aggression, that we would finally see World Peace?"

"No," said Ellie, pulling out a brochure with a beaming, turbaned gentleman on the cover. "World Peace, I'm afraid, can begin only with personal transformation."

Melissa Crane had gotten a nose stud since I'd last seen her, and had replaced Ethan with a dentist named Betsy. Like many women of her generation, Melissa informed me, she occasionally swung the other way. Gee, I thought, we'd felt liberated, way back when, just being able to swing the one way. That sexual revolution we were so proud of suddenly seemed kind of quaint.

She turned on the machine. I'd promised to talk about the notorious website today.

"It was Carole's idea," I began, "but I came up with the name, call-to-flabby-arms.com. Ellie did the graphics: Parodies of famous paintings—Mrs. American Gothic packing heat; Whistler's Mother with a mustache and bandoliers across her chest, like Pancho Villa in drag. And Janet ran the whole thing out of the computer lab at Central Community College. It was a rinky-dink operation. Just a way to share information with like-minded individuals, at least at first: How to let the air out of a tire. Care and handling of the slime gun. Solid practical stuff. Plus the occasional recipe.

It was the idea of it that struck a chord.

And ideas can take on a life of their own.

Ideas can change the world.

OK, maybe not the whole world. Maybe not even a whole block. Maybe just one ass-kicking grandma at a time.

But believe me when I say that if we had known the website would lead to the kidnapping and Jason Wolf and the rest…"

I paused.

"Yes…?" Melissa Crane leaned forward.

"Well, we probably would have done it anyway. In a nanosecond.

"But we didn't pay much attention to the website at the beginning. We had more pressing matters to take care of close to home. You've heard of Dr. Jim Sloane, I suppose."

"The plastic surgeon?" Melissa Crane said. "Who hasn't heard of Jim Sloane? You don't mean to say you were also responsible for the…"

"The most famous infomercial ever made, even more famous than Mr. Popiel? Yes, that was us, Ellie mostly and her boyfriend, Ramon, though it would never have happened if Tiffany Reed hadn't walked into my office that day, crying her heavily mascaraed eyes out…"

Chapter Three

The Case of the Surgeon Who Couldn't Cut Straight

I'd heard his ads on the radio. I'd seen his billboards. Realize your divine loveliness. Be the woman you've always wanted to be. Why settle for anything less than perfection? Visa and MasterCard accepted.

But now, for the first time, I'd gotten a peek at Dr. Sloane's handiwork.

Tiffany Reed didn't actually disrobe in my office, needless to say. She didn't have to. Just one look and you could tell she wasn't the woman she'd always wanted to be, unless the woman she wanted to be was about five foot tall, with breasts the size of volleyballs and cleavage that began just south of her chin.

He made me grotesque, she said. Or, to be precise, what she said was: "He made me, like, a fucking freak, that fucking pervert."

I studied the "before" pictures Tiffany had spread over my desk: mug shots of small, comma shaped breasts—in left profile, in right profile, from above, from below and fully frontal. They appeared to be your standard 34A's, a little prominent in the nipple maybe, but nice enough otherwise.

"They look fine to me," I said.

"That's what I told her," her boyfriend Craig chimed in. "I told her I liked them just the way they were." He was not much of a tit man, he added by way of further explanation.

"But you supported me in my decision," she reminded him.

"Of course," he mumbled.

I got the impression that Craig supported Tiffany in every decision she made, even when the decision was whether to order the large or the medium Domino's Pizza Supreme.

Then she brought out the "after" shot. This resembled not so much a bosom as an aerial photo of the Capitol dome—or rather two Capitol domes—attached to a chest wall. The nipples now pointed in opposite directions—one up, one down—as though they were signaling something in semaphore, possibly: "Help!! He made me a fucking freak, that fucking pervert."

I'd never seen anything like it.

"Tell me what happened," I said. "Briefly."

(Emphasis on the "briefly." I had Tiffany pegged as what Big Howie—that's Howard Berkowitz, my law partner—refers to as a "Michener," after the novelist James Michener, whose sweeping historical epics were extremely popular in the 1960s and who nobody but Howie reads anymore.

"The trouble with your James Michener novel," Howie likes to say, "is that he always starts the story back with molten rocks. Who gives a shit about molten rocks?" When Howie interviews a client like that, he'll cut the person short after five minutes saying, "Skip the Big Bang, please, and let's get straight to Life crawling out of the primordial ooze." There were times I wished I could be more like Big Howie.)

Tiffany's Story

Ever since Tiffany Reed had had any breasts at all, she'd longed for bigger ones, a lot bigger, but not, like, stripper big. Not, like, a total slut big.

Now Tiffany was the kind of person who, once she wanted something, she went for it. That's how she'd hooked up with her boyfriend Craig, who when he wasn't delivering packages for UPS, was a drummer in a rock band called *Scrambled Brains.* She'd seen him at a concert and thought, "Wow, he's really hot." So when her friend Allison dared her, she went right up on stage during a break and gave him her phone number.

Same thing with the operation. Once she knew she had to have it, well she just had to have it, even though it cost $6000 and she earned only $12 an hour as a hostess at the Paradise Grill. So she made a plan. She would save $100 from each paycheck till she had enough for a down payment, which would have worked out fine except something always seemed to come up. Such as she got a bad strep infection and couldn't work for a month. Or Allison talked her into going to Club Med Cancun. Or she got deeply depressed and the only thing that made her feel better was to go shopping. After a year and a half she had exactly $250 in her boob job fund. It was beginning to look like her dream would remain just that—a dream.

Then one day she heard Dr. Sloane's ad on the radio. Be everything you always wanted to be. Why settle for anything less than perfection. That really spoke to her. That expressed her whole philosophy of life. And then—most important—Visa and MasterCard accepted. Clearly this was a message from God, she thought, because as it happened, she had two credit cards that weren't maxed out yet. With what she could borrow from Craig, that would add up to almost $3000 right there, and Dr. Sloane's bookkeeper said they'd take the rest in time payments.

So she made an appointment for an evaluation at his office, which was like something out of a magazine. There was even a marble statue that the receptionist told her was supposed to be some famous goddess, but it looked to Tiffany like whoever she was, she sure could use some major liposuction.

Then the nurse gave Tiffany a form to fill out, with questions Tiffany really had to think about. Why do you want this operation? What do you hope this procedure will do for you? She remembered what that psychologist on Oprah had said. Sometimes you think, "if only I could lose ten pounds," or "if only I had tighter buns," and what you really mean is, "I want to change my life." Is this why Tiffany wanted larger breasts? Did Tiffany want to change her Life? Well she certainly didn't want to be a hostess at the Paradise Grill forever, she knew that much. She hoped to move into management one day; maybe go to Community College and get an Associate of Arts degree. The restaurant owner, Archie DuBow, encouraged her, said she was way too sharp to be spending her time seating parties of six. But of course he also wanted to fuck her, so who knows if he really meant it.

But she didn't want to go into all that, so where it said why do you want this operation, she just wrote down: "bigger boobs."

She sat and sat for about an hour, which gave her time to check out the two other patients in the waiting room. They were old, around 50 she'd guess, and rich looking: $700 handbags; designer shoes. No lines on their faces, but you could tell they were old anyway by their hands and necks and the way their shoulders slumped all forward. So what was the point, Tiffany wondered? Why spend a gazillion dollars on a facelift if everybody can tell you're old anyway? But maybe Tiffany would feel different when she got old herself. Like her mother always said, "Never judge a person till you've walked a mile in her moccasins."

Finally, after she'd sat there practically forever, the nurse called Tiffany's name and led her into the examining room and told her to take off everything but her panties. Then Dr. Sloane walked in before Tiffany could even put on the drape. It made her feel funny, but she figured, hey he's the doctor, even though her gynecologist, who was a woman, always knocked first.

Dr. Sloane sure didn't look the way she'd pictured him. He didn't look like a doctor at all—more like the dude who came to her house that time to sell her a burglar alarm after she'd put her name in a box at the mall to get a free security system, only it turned out it wasn't really free. Dr. Sloane had that same gelled-up hair, the big teeth, the cheeks shaved really close till they shined. The same small, pudgy hands that reminded her of white mice.

He sat on a stool with wheels, crossed his legs and looked deep into her eyes. We're going to make your dreams come true, he said. And he asked her to remove her panties so he could get a better sense of her total body contour. Then he took those pictures she'd showed me, but they were only from the waist up, so she didn't understand why he needed her panties off in the first place.

Then she put on a drape and they walked to the fitting

room so she could be sized, with him keeping his hand on her back the whole time.

That fitting room—wow—it had every shape and variety boob you can imagine, and Dr. Sloane said any one of them could be hers just for the asking.

So first she tries on this really nice 34 C, round and high, which she thought was just about perfect. But no, Dr. Sloane told her, to achieve the look she wanted, the look she deserved, she needed to go a little bigger.

And every size she tries on, it's the same thing. He keeps saying, "no, go bigger, go bigger," till finally she got to where it must've been like a triple E. She thought it looked way large, but he told her trust him, it was exactly right, and if she didn't like it afterwards he could always make it smaller, but if she went too small, he couldn't make it bigger. She said OK, figuring he must know, and they scheduled the operation for a month away, which would give her a chance to work a couple of extra shifts and save toward the down payment.

Then a week before the surgery, he calls her seven o'clock on a Sunday and says would she like to have dinner with him? He happened to be in her neighborhood, and he thought if she had any questions or concerns about the procedure this would give her an opportunity to share them in a more relaxed atmosphere. Studies, he said, had shown a higher probability of a favorable outcome when the patient got to know the surgeon as a person. This made sense to Tiffany, since she was aware from her own experience that the mind can have a major major influence on the body.

Craig had a gig that night, which come to think of it Sloane knew because he'd asked for the band's schedule, said he liked to keep up with what was happening on the local pop scene. Tiffany thought that was pretty funny, since the music Dr. Sloane played in his office had to be at least two hundred years old. When she mentioned this, he told her, oh that was for professional purposes only, for ambience; that what he really enjoyed was heavy metal like her friend Gregg played. *Scrambled Brains* was ska punk, she said, and Dr. Sloane said oh, he dug that too.

Now Tiffany wasn't a complete idiot. She knew that when an old dude like Sloane asks you out for an expensive dinner, it's usually because he wants to fuck you. Archie Dubow was always asking her to dinner, for instance. (Like right; like she really wanted to have dinner with Archie DuBow and his perspiration problem and the dumb jokes he got off the internet.) But she dismissed the possibility of a hidden fuck-motive with Sloane. He was her Doctor, after all. She just thought he was a genuinely caring person.

Anyway, she had nothing better to do that night and she knew he had a Ferrari, and she said to herself, wow, that would be a great story to tell Allison. Tiffany Reed in a Ferrari!

He drove way out to the suburbs to this Polynesian place with a bridge over a fish pond. It was his special dining spot, he said, and everybody there seemed to know him. And she liked that they got a really good table with a view of the pond, and that Dr. Sloane (who by this time she was calling Jim) ordered five different appetizers just to start, each one totally delicious. Plus a whole bottle of Chardonnay after she told him that was her favorite wine. (When she and Craig went out to dinner, which wasn't that often, he had a hissy fit if she got anything besides the main entrée.)

She really enjoyed the conversation too, which surprised her because she'd wondered what they'd have to talk about. But he put her at ease right away, asking questions about her hopes, her ambitions. She told him about wanting to get an Associate's degree in hotel and restaurant management. He said he admired her for taking control of her life, knowing what she wanted and going for it (which happened to be what she liked best about herself). And he told her how cosmetic surgery wasn't just about the money for him, it was about making people feel better about themselves, which was why he planned to go to Romania to operate on orphans with cleft palates, which made them complete outcasts in their society. Wow, Tiffany thought. She wished she had a skill like that, a skill that could benefit deformed children.

After he paid the check (it was more than Tiffany earned in a whole Saturday night shift), he asked if she'd mind if they stopped at his office on the way back, so he could pick up some files he needed to study before tomorrow's procedures.

Well by the time they got to the office, Tiffany was feeling pretty hammered, a lot more hammered than she usually got from one bottle of wine. So hammered, Sloane had to help her into the elevator and she had to lean against him just to stand up. He smelled good, she remembered, like cucumbers.

She couldn't remember much else about the next hour. She might have taken her top off and posed with the statue of the fat lady. Then there might have been something about nitrous oxide. But that all could've been her imagination or a dream. Because she definitely did fall asleep, and the next thing she knew Dr. Jim was shaking her and telling her he had to get some coffee in her and get her home and that he had to get home himself, or his wife would be having a hissy fit.

Then on the day of the operation he was strictly business, a little cold and distant even, as though they'd never shared hopes and ambitions and five Hawaiian-style appetizers. It reminded her of how it is the next day when you fuck a guy drunk who you don't really like and who doesn't really like you. But maybe she was being overly sensitive, and this was just his professional demeanor. She wanted to believe that. Like her mother said, give people the benefit of the doubt.

Well she got pretty upset when she woke from the anesthesia and she had these *humongous things* on her chest with the nips pointing the wrong way, but he told her it was only the post-surgical swelling and she needed to wait for things to settle down.

She waited, and waited. But two months later when the boobs were still this huge, Craig said if it bothered her, she should go back and tell Sloane to make them smaller, like he promised. And to do something about the nipples while he was in there anyway.

What seems to be the problem? Sloane smiled at her with those big teeth. You look fantastic. And when she told him she wanted the boobs smaller, like he promised, he said sure, but it would cost her another $3000 and she still owed him $1500 for the first operation. As for the nipples, they were that way before, only now that the boobs were bigger the nipples appeared more so, like when you blow up a balloon. Was it his fault she had a genetic flaw?

Tiffany cried every morning as soon as she woke up and saw herself in the mirror over the bed. She cried a lot during the day too, and at night before she went to sleep. She no longer felt good about herself. Finally Craig couldn't stand it any more, so he talked to Joe Solomon, the shop steward, who knew a lot about the law, and Solomon said to stop making payments immediately, which Tiffany did. Next thing, she starts getting these calls from a collection agency calling her a deadbeat and a loser and they added on all these fees and interest until now the bill was almost double. And Craig said, fuck it, let's just sue the fucking bastard.

My old friend Joe Solomon gave them my name and here they were. Would I take the case on a contingent fee, Tiffany wanted to know, a percentage of whatever the jury gave her? She didn't really care about the money. She just wanted to see justice done.

Who doesn't? If only it were that simple! As Big Howie likes to say, you can't pay the overhead with a one-third cut of justice. Which is why you have to be careful, Howie also likes to say, to sue only the right kind of bastard: specifically a bastard with a weak defense, a credibility problem, and a deep pocket.

So we had agreed to agree before taking on a potentially expensive and time-consuming case, like this one.

"I'll discuss it with my partner," I told them. Though I could already guess Howie wouldn't think Sloane was our kind of SOB.

Howie Berkowitz wiped his bifocals with his 1970 vintage tie, transferring a speck of yolk to one lens in the process. He pinched the grimy clot of adhesive on the earpiece.

"I told Renee this would hold if we doubled the scotch tape. Look at that...practically perfect."

"You can afford a new pair of glasses," I said, irritated, knowing that he was stalling, fumbling with those antique spectacles of his so he wouldn't have to say no, and we wouldn't get into another one of our big arguments over principle.

"That's not the point," Howie replaced the glasses on the bridge of his substantial nose. "They don't make this style frame anymore. Probably they'll never make this style frame again. Not ever."

Years ago, Howie's wife Renee, who is a therapist, had given up trying to convince Howie to buy anything manufactured since the heyday of the Beatles. It's Howie's way of dealing with the inevitability of change, and loss, and ultimately with Death itself, Renee claims, and considers it a relatively healthy response to the fundamental paradox of the Human Condition. Healthy, at least compared to being an alcoholic, which had been Howie's other main way of dealing with the human condition, before he'd met Renee.

"I think he drugged her unconscious and then had sex with her," I said. "That's what I think."

Howie leaned back in his chair.

"Which you intend to prove exactly how? With the word of a waitress maxed out on her credit cards against the word of a plastic surgeon with a billboard on Route 28, a man with a red Ferrari, a man who, face it, can get all the regular wide-awake poontang any man could possibly want or need. So why would he bother? That's what the jury's gonna ask itself. Why would he even bother?"

"Maybe that's how he likes it. Maybe it makes him feel totally in control."

"Yeah—well, most guys prefer a woman who at least *pretends* to be moving. At least that's how the jury's gonna see it."

This was a pretty simple-minded view of the male sexual urge, in my opinion, especially coming from Howie, who had once represented Eddie Wu, the city's premier smut peddler, in a landmark free speech case. Eddie maintains a database of customer preferences so he can alert his clients when anything new shows up in their kink of choice. I seemed to recollect an entire category called "Sleeping Beauties," featuring coffins, randy dentists and off-label uses for novocain.

"Plus I suspect our friend Dr. Sloane has some kind of unhealthy fixation on mammoth breasts."

Howie snorted.

"You mean unlike 97% of the straight male population? Tell me the man has sex with gerbils, you might get my attention."

Howie shook his head. I knew what he was going to say.

But I didn't care if Sloane was the wrong kind of bastard for our firm. He was the right kind for me. Besides, what did Howie know about mammoth breast fixations? I needed to consult an expert.

Yes, Eddie Wu said, a little defensively, sure he have customers who like to see ladies with giant busts. Why not? All protected by First Amendment, what consenting adults do in private of home no business of government. As intended by Founding Fathers. God bless America. That's why he came here from Taiwan in the first place. For the freedom of expression.

Yes, sure he can send me a typical example.

Two days later *Titanic Titties* arrived at my office. I called the others.

"Seven o'clock, my house," I said, "I'll provide the popcorn."

Opening shot: Big breasted woman on all fours, being penetrated from behind by muscular "Slade" on the deck of a large cabin cruiser floating among styrofoam icebergs. The words

Titanic Titties

flash across the screen. Slade grunts. Same woman performing oral sex on Slade. (Fade out)

(Fade in): Slade (looking bored): You got a nice ass, but your tits are too small. I need to find me the woman with the biggest tits on the entire planet.

And so begins his quest, which will take him all over the world, or at least all over a back yard in the San Fernando Valley tricked out to resemble the world. He will have many adventures with women of many ethnicities, all with bosoms the approximate size of yurts, and who all have nothing better to do with their spare time than to mate doggy-style with Slade, to perform oral sex on Slade, etc.

And throughout his wanderings. Slade hears rumors of a mysterious plastic surgeon known only as "Dr. Bigbooby," who is said to have mastered the secret of creating so-called "titanic titties." Our hero is determined to find him, even though everyone who seeks Bigbooby disappears and is never seen again exactly like a certain well-known luxury liner which was supposed to be unsinkable!

Undaunted, plucky Slade tracks Bigbooby to a small island off Tierra del Fuego where the doctor has created a harem of mammary freaks, who live as his sex slaves in a pine-paneled rec room (tricked out to resemble Hitler's bunker).

Slade liberates the sex slaves, and turns Bigbooby over to the proper authorities. Then everybody—including those same authorities and their handcuffs—has a down-home orgy to celebrate. The End.

"Atrocious camera work," Ellie sniffed, "really low production values."

"Repetitive. Weak on character development," Janet added.

Carole waved her hand.

"That updating of the *Odyssey* thing, which I suppose is what they were trying for; that mythic hero's journey, a la Joseph Campbell, by way of Jung, it's been done before and much, much better."

But that wasn't the point.

"You think this might be a case of Life imitating non-Art?" Carole said.

I had given each of them a dossier on Dr. Sloane, summarizing my paralegal's investigation into his background.

"He's done business in four other states so far. Roars into town with his billboards and radio ads, sets up a fancy office; does a high volume business—mainly in boobs. Clears out one step ahead of the malpractice suits: two in Texas, two in Florida, one in Mississippi. Same general complaint. Grossly oversized breasts on small women. Odd deformities. Possible hanky-panky. Only the suits never go anywhere, because the women back down, or they can't get another doctor to testify that Sloane did anything wrong. Or their lawyers decide it's too much trouble to chase a guy who's moved halfway across the country by then on a case they probably can't win.

"So it looks like it's up to us to stop him, ladies, before he cuts again," I said.

And that's when we came up with the plan....

"Dear Dr. Sloane, (the letter read):

How would you like to quadruple your business? Gain national exposure at a minimal cost? Become a household name?

Before you say no, please take just five minutes to read this letter.

I am a public relations professional, and as soon as I saw your recent 30-second advertisement on late night television, I knew you had a message which really spoke to today's woman: Be everything you can be.

Yes—Be everything you can be, Dr. Sloane.

Because I believe you have genuine guru quality. And that with the right promotional campaign, you could become the Wayne Dyer of breast enlargement, the Suze Orman of liposuction. How will you accomplish this? I'll say it in one word...

Infomercial..."

Sloane had been intrigued by the letter, he had to admit, particularly because he'd been thinking along those lines himself, and also because she'd offered to do all the production work practically free, just to demonstrate her faith in his potential to make it really big.

So now here she was in his office, a large, imposing woman with extraordinary breasts, like two great ripe watermelons, though watermelons badly in need of lift and separation. They should jut, he thought, and perhaps in her long-ago youth they had, but by now they merely billowed. In ten years, if she wasn't careful, they'd be dugs, great limp sacks flapping down around her waist, like a Russian grandmother's. Time did terrible things to the female body, as who knew better than Sloane.

"An Infomercial?" he asked.

"But tasteful," she said, "no abrasive pitchmen; no 800 numbers flashing on the screen. You're not selling a better way to chop carrots; you're selling a dream."

Maybe start out with a soft-focus shot of the Taj Mahal; the Venus de Milo. Then the theme—why settle for anything less than perfection? Then Sloane himself explaining the many options open to today's woman seeking to be the best she could be; a few carefully chosen before and after pics. Then the theme again: Perfection—because you're worth it.

These were just ideas she was throwing around, she said. The details could be worked out later. The point to get across was that cosmetic surgery isn't just about superficial appearances. What you do is so important, she said; you make people feel better about themselves. All most doctors can do for people is to keep them from feeling even worse about themselves.

Yes, that was it exactly, he thought. All most doctors can do for people is to keep them from feeling even worse about themselves. He'd have to remember that the next time some self-righteous oncologist looked down on him because Sloane wasn't trying to cure cancer; or when some public health type wondered how a person could spend his whole life catering to the shallow vanity of the rich. As though there were anything shallow about vanity. As though it weren't practically the deepest impulse of the human heart...

And vanity isn't exclusively for the wealthy either, Sloane knew. In Sloane's experience those of modest means could be just as appearance-conscious as your higher socioeconomic brackets. This was why Sloane allowed his patients to pay over time, though Rita, his bookkeeper, said it was an accounting nightmare. Sloane believed that voluptuous breasts or a flat stomach should be available to everyone, regardless of income or social class. If that made him some kind of radical, so be it...

He explained this to the Big Woman, who really seemed to comprehend, to take it in. She was a good listener, he thought. He would have liked to curl up against her, his head pillowed on that welcoming chest, and tell her all about his hopes and dreams and ambitions. And then suck her gigantic tits…

Sometimes you had to make a leap of faith. That's what he told his patients, and now that's what he told himself.

"An infomercial—why not?"

He smiled at the woman (who had really excellent skin for a gal her age). What did he have to lose?

(Except, as it turned out, everything.)

"I could tell just by the way he looked at me," Ellie said, when we met at her house the next night, "that he had major issues around people of size."

Ramon passed around plates of his homemade empanadas, and set a pitcher of his secret family recipe sangria on the glass coffee table. Ellie had let him move into her basement when he'd been evicted from his furnished room, and he'd turned out to be an ideal housemate, a person of varied and surprising talents. He was an excellent cook. He could repair small appliances. He knew his way around a computer. And he'd once produced and directed a short documentary about the life cycle of a refrigerator, from its shiny beginnings on thc assembly line to its abandonment in a junkyard on the outskirts of an urban slum. It had been a metaphor for his country's history, he said, and it had won a prize at some obscure festival on some minor continent. Unfortunately, *Fridgedairio* had failed to receive widespread distribution, and so here Ramon was, volunteering to be both director and cinematographer on the project we'd code-named: "Go Plastic."

"He don't know what he's missing babe," Ramon leered at Ellie in a way I found oddly endearing.

"He talked to my chest the entire time," Ellie said. "What a total waste of makeup."

Sloane had telephoned Ellie the morning after their meeting; said he'd been up all night jotting down ideas. How would she like to meet him for dinner at the Hilo House to brainstorm. Did she know the place—the one with the tiki torches and the curved bridge over the fishpond?

Ramon frowned.

"He tries anything funny...," Ramon made a slicing gesture with his right hand, "so long *cojones.*"

"I doubt it'll come to that," Ellie said. "I doubt a man like Sloane sees me as a woman at all."

Nevertheless, Ramon followed Ellie to the Hilo House, just in case. Or rather, since he had no transportation of his own, he made the trip in the back seat of Ellie's Honda, ducking down when they got to the parking lot, so Sloane wouldn't spot him. From this vantage point, he studied Sloane as the doctor emerged from the red Ferrari. An individual who wears shades at night, Ramon noticed; a buff individual who obviously puts in time working out at the gym. But buff or no, Ramon knew he could take this individual in a fair fight; that Ramon would make up in fierceness, cunning and skill for whatever he might lack in raw muscle.

Of course, Ramon reflected, it probably never would come to any kind of fight at all. Or if it did, his Big Momma could squash the doctor like a bug. It was one of the things he loved about her—that she could take care of herself, and so he would never be called upon to prove his manhood for her sake.

He'd proven his manhood once, long ago, with disastrous results, and hoped never to have to repeat the experience:

Ramon's Story

When he was a small boy—the smallest in his village—larger boys were always proving their own manhoods by beating up on Ramon. For not only was Ramon small, Ramon hated to fight. He hated the crunch of fist on bone (his). He hated the crack of knuckle on jaw (his). Most of all he hated the sight of blood on shirt (his). So Ramon usually just tried to get the beating-up part over with as quickly as possible, by falling down after the first swing, and playing dead.

After a while the other boys realized there wasn't much point in beating up on Ramon, because it proved exactly nothing, least of all your manhood. Who couldn't beat up on Ramon? Even a girl could probably beat up on Ramon, if she really wanted.

So the boys left him alone, and this was fine with him. He didn't mind that he had few friends, and that those few tended to be the village losers, like Pablo Martinez, who wore thick glasses and once wet his pants in math class. Ramon didn't mind, because he had hopes and dreams for a better life. He was the smartest kid in his entire grade, and the nuns at the mission school told him he could go to University one day and become anything he wanted to be. Did that include a movie director in Hollywood, Ramon asked, (because that's what he really wanted to be), and Sister Mary Elizabeth crossed herself, and said no, *Madre de Dios*, she meant an engineer.

Well, becoming an engineer was good enough, Ramon thought, so long as it got him out of the village, with its constant manhood-proving. Meanwhile, he continued to drop at the first swing and play dead, and the others continued to leave him alone, and everything was going along just fine.

Until the terrible day Tomas da Vila moved to town.

Tomas was different from the other boys. While the other boys beat people up to prove something, Tomas beat people up just because he enjoyed beating people up. He liked to hear the crunch of fist on bone, the crack of knuckle on jaw. Most of all he loved the sight of other people's blood, especially Ramon's.

And when Ramon took his usual fall after Tomas' first swing, Tomas, instead of backing off in disgust and calling Ramon a girly-girl (like a normal boy would've), kicked Ramon's head, and then he twisted Ramon' s arm until Ramon almost fainted from the pain.

Ramon tried avoiding Tomas, but Tomas would hunt him down in order to punch him in the stomach or give him a wrist burn or a nosebleed. Ramon tried bribing Tomas with the delicious empanadas and *arroz con pollo* Ramon's mother stuffed in his lunchbox. (Tomas' family was very poor, and he usually brought only a tortilla and a few beans for lunch; sometimes he brought nothing.) But soon Tomas began to complain about the monotony of the menu. How come your mama never makes beefsteak ranchero, he'd say, swatting Ramon on the side of the head. How come all I ever get are your leftovers, bending Ramon's finger back till it practically broke.

Then one day Ramon forgot his lunchbox, and Tomas got so angry he ground Ramon's face into the dirt, splintering a tooth; and Tomas pulled Ramon's pants down and made him lie there while everybody came over to look.

Finally Ramon had had enough. No more Mr. Nice Guy.

Papa, he said, take me to see Tio Pepe.

This was the same Tio Pepe who had been a famous flyweight boxer in his day, and once had offered to teach Ramon the manly art of self-defense. There comes a time *muchacho*, the fighter had told him, when a person can no longer just lie down and play dead.

Now that time had come. Ramon moved into Pepe's house in a neighboring village, to learn what Pepe had to teach, which was less about beating up than not being beaten, though the world being what it is, the two often turned out to be one and the same.

Ramon proved to be an apt pupil. While he lacked a certain natural viciousness (in Pepe's opinion), he was clever, light on his feet, and very hard-working. Fighting was not about brute force anyway, Pepe told Ramon, it was about brains and grace and outwitting your opponent. Float like a butterfly, he said, sting like a bee.

One morning, about six months into the lessons, Pepe watched Ramon dance and float and shred a punching bag as if it were a pinata. "Hola!" the old boxer beamed, clapping Ramon on Ramon's newly muscled back. "You are an *hombre* now. Time to go home to mama."

Oh, Ramon was nervous that first day back at school. He clutched his lunchbox close to his chest, and winced when Tomas loomed in front of him at recess. "Why look who's here," Tomas sneered, his brittle wolfish teeth clenching in an evil grin. "I've missed you, girly girl."

The other boys surrounded them, eyes glazed with juvenile bloodlust. "Break his nose Tomas," one shouted. "Kick his sorry butt," another yelled.

Their champion clasped his hands over his head and

pirouetted in a (somewhat premature, as it turned out) victory dance. He rested a sweaty palm on Ramon's trembling head, and drew back his other fist. "Uno, dos...." he began. But before Tomas had gotten to 'tres' (and the limit of his mathematical knowledge), Ramon whirled like Pepe had taught him, and as Tomas swung haplessly at the air, Ramon floated like a butterfly.

And then Ramon stung like a bee, knocking the bigger boy to the ground with one swift left to the jaw; one quick right to the solar plexus. Tomas lay there silent, playing dead. Or so Ramon thought. And this is the part that was painful for Ramon to remember. Because Tomas wasn't just playing dead, Tomas actually *was* dead, having hit his head on a rock on the way down, shattering his thick skull, oozing the few brains he had out into the red village dirt.

It was enough to make Ramon lose his taste for fisticuffs right then and there. And ever since, he'd avoided situations where he might be called on once again to prove his manhood. Manhood, he'd decided, could be hazardous to a person's health.

So he had no intention of fighting the doctor. No. That's not why he was here. He was here to make sure that she didn't decide to get into the doctor's fancy car and let the doctor drive her someplace where the doctor could play with her big titties and all the other big beautiful things about her. He doesn't think of me as a woman, she'd said, but Ramon didn't believe that was possible. And because Ellie was a woman, he knew she would be susceptible to the charms of red Ferraris and fancy sunglasses, no matter that she had told him many times that she valued experiences more than she valued things.

Which was lucky for Ramon. Ramon couldn't afford to give women things, so experiences is what he gave them instead. He thought of courtship as a kind of low-budget film, relying heavily on outdoor locations and the creative use of inexpensive props. Scene One: They meet for coffee. He offers her a single blossom which he'd liberated from a nearby cemetery. Scene Two: A beach at twilight. A candle. A stolen bottle of Chianti. A little Neruda in the original. A little Neruda in translation. They kiss. Scene Three: Hot sex in an offbeat setting. Choose the spot carefully. Public enough to be free of charge, yet secluded enough to avoid arrest for indecent exposure: The fitting room at The Gap. A stalled elevator in an office building. Late at night on the back seat of a city bus.

No, Ramon wasn't here to fight the doctor. Ramon was here because he was in love. He had no idea how it had happened. When he'd posted that profile seeking a big beautiful woman for fun and games, maybe more, Love wasn't the "more" he'd had in mind. He'd hoped at best for a sham marriage which would get him a green card, so he could work in Hollywood, instead of picking up the odd dishwashing job.

But there she was, his Ellie, so pillowy, so undulating, her creamy skin tinged with pale peach like that flower he'd given her at their first meeting. Truly, he thought, he'd come to the Promised Land…

Ramon adored many things about America, but most of all he adored the largeness of its ladies. Fifty percent of them were over size 16, according to the newspapers, which seemed to consider this a problem, and urged readers to consume more fruits and vegetables, and say no to the dessert cart. Or live on nothing but special diet drinks and sliced grapefruit. It could be a cruel country, he thought, especially to its women, who not only were expected to survive on chalky beverages tasting of old socks, but were supposed to do so while running in place on a giant machine for 45 minutes a day. All so they could become firm.

American men, it seemed, prized firmness above everything else in women. Ramon sometimes wondered how a country full of such men had ever managed to become a great imperial power. You should be able to sink into a woman like a featherbed, or a great mound of fluffy mashed potatoes. In his native land, everybody understood this. He'd tried a firm woman once, and it had been like making love to a scale model of the solar system—all knobs and odd protrusions everywhere, and getting jabbed in the belly by a moon of Jupiter during the supreme moment of passion.

Oh God of Love, give him a Big woman any day, who generally feels bad about herself (according to American television), and consequently pays for dinner and doesn't have unrealistic expectations as to his fidelity. And when he whispers that she is beautiful, (and means it), her eyes go all moist with gratitude, and Ramon knows that the world is a better, a kinder place because he passed through.

Not Ellie, though. Ellie wasn't grateful to him at all. She'd made it clear right from the beginning, that she was the one doing him the favor, not the other way around.

He had little to offer her, he knew. No money. No real job. No social position. Only his dream of making it one day in the movie business. And they couldn't live on dreams. Which was why it was so convenient that Ellie had that trust fund, though he was sure he would have liked her nearly as well even without it.

He squirmed in the narrow back seat of the Honda Civic. It couldn't help the cause of his love, he thought, that she was in there having dinner with a rich and important man right now, a doctor, a man who, Ellie admitted, couldn't take his eyes off her chest.

Damn the man to Hell!

Not exactly Dr. Jim's usual piece of cupcake, the maitre d' thought. Business, not pleasure, he decided, and seated them at a quiet table in the nearly empty back room, far from the pointlessly seductive glow of the tiki lamps; the needless sensuality of the golden koi. Dr. Jim wouldn't want the woman getting the wrong idea.

The maitre d' took good care of Jim. The plastic surgeon, the one from the billboards, was a frequent customer, and tipped him well. Bribed you well you mean, the maitre d's wife would laugh. Discretion mattered to the patrons of the Hilo House, mainly well-to-do married men out with lovely young ladies they introduced as their nieces visiting from Portland or Cincinnati.

And because Dr. Jim was such a good customer, and also because the maitre d' was curious to know what Jim was doing there with such an un-cupcake of a woman, the maitre d' passed by their table twice, inquiring how everything was, and whether the fresh mahi-mahi he'd recommended had lived up to expectations.

That's how he happened to see the pictures spread out all over their table: naked female body parts, improved and unimproved; the improved ones spectacular in their unnatural perfection. So later, when some of these same body parts showed up in the notorious infomercial, the maitre d' could tell his wife that, in a way, he'd been there at the very beginning, if only he'd known it. He liked to impress his wife, who was considerably younger than he, with accounts of the celebrities who dined at the Hilo House incognito (or so they thought): the ex-Senator; the weatherman from Channel Four; that actor whose name he couldn't remember, who'd been on that series whose name he couldn't remember either. The maitre d's wife had grown up in a small town on the other side of the mountains, and these brushes with the near-great made her feel connected to something larger than herself, some world of people whose lives mattered in a way hers never had and never would.

But what the maitre d' remembered best about that night wasn't the pictures, it was the peculiar incident in the parking lot afterwards. It was late, near closing time, when Sloane and his companion left. The maitre d' had walked them to the door, so he saw the whole thing: Sloane climbing into the Ferrari; the woman getting in next to him; Sloane leaning over the woman to fasten her seat belt; then this long-haired person in a muumuu streaking across the lot, waving an umbrella, shouting something about "Cohens," banging on the windshield; the big woman leaping out, fast and agile for her size; grabbing the attacker; hauling the attacker by the neck over to a small car; tossing the attacker inside; driving off.

What could it have been about, he asked his wife later, shaking his head. He liked to bring home incidents from work for her to mull over. It gave them something to talk about.

Maybe it was the doctor's wife, driven mad by jealousy, she said. Or maybe, the maitre d' said, remembering that shouted "Cohens," some crazed anti-Semite striking out at a supposed symbol of Hebrew wealth. Not that the maitre d' thought Sloane was a Jew. What self-respecting Jew would drive one of those monstrosities, with their terrible gas mileage?

"Ramon almost spoiled the whole thing, doing his Norman Bates in drag routine," Ellie said. "I told Sloane it was just my cross-dressing brother gone off his medication again."

"He was grabbing at your mangoes," Ramon shrugged.

"Fastening my seat belt," Ellie laughed. "Fastening my seat belt. He wanted to take me for a ride. Impress me. And then Ramon comes banging on the windshield, yelling he's gonna slice off Sloane's *cojones*. With an umbrella."

Janet, Carole and I looked at each other. Were they were thinking what I was thinking: when was the last time a man had threatened to castrate someone for our sakes? It certainly wasn't the kind of thing I could imagine Carole's husband Henry doing, for instance, pale silent Henry who disappeared into his workshop whenever the book group met at Carole's house. What does he do down there, I asked Carole once. He rearranges his tools, Carole said, it helps him relax. Relax from what, I wondered—his habitual torpor? And as for Janet's Eric, the professor of social work, this was a man who swerved to avoid large spiders in the road.

I wondered if Ellie appreciated what she had in Ramon.

"First thing," Ramon pounded his fist on the coffee table,

"is I need total creative control. That the doctor has to be made to understand right from the beginning."

Carole rolled her eyes.

"It's a phony infomercial, Ramon, not *Citizen Kane*."

Carole didn't have much patience with Ramon's artistic vision or its associated costs. Sloane was paying us only $5000 for production, which, according to Ramon, wasn't enough to make a first-rate bar mitzvah video, much less a short subject headed for national distribution. Ramon had begun complaining about the budgetary constraints before we'd even shot our first second of footage. He might not have the talent to become a great Hollywood director, but he certainly had the temperament.

Budgetary constraints aside, the actual production of the infomercial was going to be the easy part. The real challenge would be switching the tapes so our version was the one which would go out over the airwaves in ten major media markets. Ramon said it could be done. He would use his knowledge of the inside workings of a television station to do it.

I didn't know whether to believe him, about knowing the inside workings of a television station, that is. If Ramon had done half the things he claimed to have done, by my calculations he would be about 94 years old, and would have gotten his first job before he was toilet-trained.

On the other hand, what did we have to lose? If it didn't work, millions would see an infomercial for a boob job mill. Millions would forget it. But if it did work—ah if it did work...

You had to smile just thinking about it.

We hired a service which guaranteed it would deliver the "corrected" tapes exactly two hours before the scheduled broadcast. The station would never bother to run the tape all the way through that close to air time, Ramon said. There's only a skeleton staff there during the "paid programming," and everything gets done on the cheap.

To: Advertising Department, KQPX (the note read):

Dear Fred,

Whoops! The tape we sent you last week with the infomercial, "Be Everything You Can Be," had the wrong phone number at the end... can you believe it? Enclosed is the corrected version. So sorry to spring this on you at the very last minute. We regret any inconvenience this may have caused.

BGFH Productions

Sloane paced back and forth in his tastefully furnished den, pausing only to refill his snifter from the bottle of Remy Martin on the antique mahogany bar. He had tried to relax, breathing deeply to center himself the way the Big Woman had taught him, but it was no use, not tonight. Soon he would leave for the restaurant where he was hosting the launch party, and then at 1 AM the infomercial would be broadcast in ten major media markets. How could he relax?

It had seemed a crazy idea when she'd first suggested it, to run ads in ten cities, though he had just the one office right here in town. But she explained how the whole purpose of an infomercial was to stimulate demand, demand he would need if he were ever going to realize his dream—the nationwide chain of boob job mills which she referred to as "Tits R Us," (though the actual name would be "The Sloane Centers for Aesthetic Enhancement").

Think Big, she'd said, destiny didn't come cheap. And she'd talked him into taking out a large bank loan, way more than he could afford, to purchase all that airtime.

He hoped she was right. He knew his judgment was clouded where the Big Woman was concerned. She had some kind of hold on him, he wasn't sure why. Maybe it was because he'd realized from the minute he saw her that she could be his masterpiece—a monumental work on a large canvas, his Sistine Chapel, his Guernica. She'd laughed when he told her that, and claimed she was happy with herself the way she was. Sloane knew this couldn't possibly be true. Women were like that, forever saying "no no no" when they meant "yes yes yes." After a while, a man learns to just ignore the "no no no" and assume the "yes yes yes."

An assumption easier to make, Sloane had found, when the woman in question happened to be unconscious.

He'd discovered this by accident that first time, eight years ago, with a sexy little exotic dancer named Sharowna Delight, who'd gotten a nice set of Triple F's for professional purposes. She had flirted with him during the consultation, talked dirty, used not only the "f" word, but even the "c" word, so he could tell both that she was no lady and that she wanted him bad. Consequently, he had been a little surprised when she 'd rejected his dinner invitation, but it turned out that once again no no no meant yes yes yes.

The anesthetic had taken longer than usual to wear off, and his nurse had gone home early—some family obligation—so Sloane found himself alone with the still out-of-it Sharowna. He'd always felt an almost maternal tenderness toward sleeping women, and he began to cover her with one of the soft wool blankets the nurse kept handy in the recovery room. Then he noticed that Sharowna was sleeping on her back with her legs flung wide apart, body language which said to Sloane louder than any words—yes yes yes, do me, do me, f*** me, f*** me.

And so he had.

After that, it had been hard to go back to regular wide-awake women with their demands for mutual satisfaction, their expectations of post-coital conversation, their occasional criticisms of his performance or equipment. He'd had some qualms, at first. He knew sex with patients was frowned on by the medical establishment. But he only did it once in a while, only with the slutty ones no one would believe anyway, and the women always woke up with lovely happy smiles on their faces and no memory of how the smiles had gotten there, so he figured, where was the harm?

He refilled the glass, and toasted himself in the mirror over the bar.

"To dreams, and to making them come true."

And to the Big Woman, his muse, who had made it all possible.

Could a man ask for a greater happiness than this, Ramon thought? To be lying naked next to an equally naked Ellie on 600-thread-count black satin sheets, having recently made love, and almost certain to make love again afterwards, one hand cradling her breast, the other poised over the remote, waiting for the grandfather clock to strike one and the broadcast to begin.

Ramon supposed he should be nervous. No one but Ramon had seen the final cut of "Be Everything You Can Be." And in a few moments, it would be seen by millions all over the country. But Ramon was not nervous. For Ramon had the unshakeable confidence that comes with knowing that he had created a masterpiece of its kind. (Granted, his competition in this genre included "The Amazing Weed Whacker," and "Orange Plus: the only bowl cleaner you'll ever need.")

Bong!

He pointed the remote, clicked. Ellie sat up against the oversized European goose down pillows, and gave his hand an encouraging squeeze, as the screen exploded with:

Image of Mount Fuji at twilight morphing softly into the Mona Lisa, who dissolves into the Taj Mahal, which becomes a Godiva chocolate truffle, out of which bursts the Venus on the half shell, all to the musical accompaniment of a Brahms concerto for violin.

"Perfection," a voice intones. "Why settle for anything less?"

"Nice," Ellie said, "very nice,"

Ramón nodded, turned up the volume.

Sloane strolls past a wall of before and after photos, the camera following.

"While we can't always promise you perfection at the Centers for Aesthetic Enhancement, we promise you'll be the best you can be."

Ramon glanced at the clock. The beginning of both versions was the same. But in exactly one minute and forty-three seconds, he'd know if the substitution had worked. As extra insurance, this morning he did something he hadn't done since he was a boy. He went to Mass and lit a candle.

Sloane sits at his desk. Framed diplomas and testimonials hang on the wall behind him.

Sloane leans forward, hands clasped.

"In my twenty years as a cosmetic surgeon, I've helped thousands of women just like you obtain the contours they always wanted. Next year a quarter-million women will opt for breast enlargement. Shouldn't you be one of them? Why settle for what nature gave you, when in a few hours you can feel more attractive, more confident, more desirable. I'll show you how."

Ramon sat up.

Here it comes, he said.

He crossed his fingers and prayed.

James Sloane M.D. piled his plate with plump boiled shrimp, teriyaki chicken wings, and some of those little fried dumplings the Hilo House did so well. He'd reserved the whole restaurant for the late-night launch party. And worth every penny too, he thought, looking around. Everybody who mattered had shown up: Todd Allworthy, president of New Hibernia Bank, which Sloane was counting on to finance the Centers for Aesthetic Enhancement; Mo Green, editor of the

Daily Beacon; Anna Yang, from the State Medical Society. Plus an assortment of his fellow cosmetic surgeons, who, Sloane was aware, looked down on him for the billboards and the radio spots. Well, let them scoff now, as they watched Sloane become a World Class Player (the Big Woman's words).

He checked his Patek Phillipe heirloom-quality watch. Five minutes to one. Sloane was nervous, but not really. That Garcia truly had produced a masterpiece of its kind: visually stunning, understated, screaming Class, Capital C. "Be Everything You Can Be" was to the ordinary run of paid programming as *Citizen Kane* was to *Attack of the Killer Tomatoes*. Sure, Miguel Garcia had been a temperamental son of a bitch, even squeezed an extra $5,000 out of Sloane for "editing." But an artist. A real artist. Sloane had watched the tape a dozen times now, each time with the same thrill of proprietary pleasure.

The maitre d' dimmed the lights and clicked on the 52" TV Sloane had rented for the occasion. Sloane relished the choral GASP at the spectacular opening sequence. Nice touch, the Venus bursting out of the chocolate. Neo–Surrealism, Garcia had called it. On the edge.

Then—Sloane talking to the camera, looking, Garcia had said, like a young Ronald Reagan. Charismatic, yet dignified…dignified enough even for Allworthy, Sloane hoped. It was because of Allworthy, who wore a Jesus-fish lapel pin, that Sloane reluctantly had insisted that Garcia cover up the nipples on the boob shots...

Sloane now sneaked a peek at the banker to check his reaction, and could tell at once that something had gone horribly wrong. The man looked as if he were about to have a cerebral hemorrhage. "What's the meaning of this Sloane," Allworthy roared, holding one hand to his throat and the other over the eyes of his wife. Shit. Sloane knew it had been a mistake to let Garcia go with the Wonderbra...

But it wasn't just Allworthy. Even Mo Greene, a seasoned old newspaper hand, and no prude, stared at Sloane, shook his head and muttered, "now I've seen fucking everything."

The others sat in stunned silence.

Sloane looked up at the screen.

And realized life as he knew it was over.

Garcia, the bastard, had made one "final edit," just like he'd promised. The director's cut.

Sloane: Like these women you can feel more attractive, more desirable. I'll show you how:

Cut to: large-breasted woman on all fours being mounted by hunky porn star with Sloane's face.

Sloane/Slade: You got a nice ass, but your tits are too small.

Cut to: Native drums. Montage; Topless tribeswomen; Indian fertility goddesses; Baywatch; South Beach in high season.

Cut to: Sloane/Slade doing women of many ethnicities, all with bosoms the approximate size of yurts.

Voiceover: All through history there is one thing men have always desired and women have always prized:

(Title superimposed on montage of gargantuan breasts)

TITANIC TITTIES

Howie Berkowitz hated having the Friday night game at Eddie Wu's. One of Eddie's six TVs was always on, sometimes all of them at once. Even when you went to take a crap, you had to do it to ESPN. Howie didn't understand people who kept the television on, but didn't watch it, like it was some kind of animated wallpaper. Besides, the ambient buzz distracted Howie from his play—not that focus mattered much when you were up against Eddie, arguably the most inept poker player Howie had ever known. The smut peddler had only a vague grasp of the basic principles of the game, to the point where he would yell "mah-jongg" when he showed a rare winning hand.

Eddie had folded for once, and was staring listlessly at the big screen when he suddenly jumped up, and began screeching, "Infringed! I been infringed."

Howie followed Eddie's eyes. "Holy shit," Howie whistled. "I think I know that guy. The doc from the billboards."

Art Demopolis also looked up.

"Yeah. And I think I know those tits. From the Lusty Lady."

There is one thing women have always desired and men have always prized:

Titanic Titties

Voiceover: Only until recently, there was little medical science could offer. Enhancement techniques were crude and frequently ineffective.

Cut to: teen in poodle skirt stuffing tissues into bra.

Cut to: falsies floating out of bathing suit top. Camera lingers on twin mounds; soft fade into icebergs.

Voiceover: And then thanks to the genius of a few determined pioneers, the implant was invented, and it changed the way we thought about breasts forever.

Cut to: Sloane, sitting at desk with hands folded: "In my twenty years as a cosmetic surgeon, I have helped thousands of women become everything they could be...."

Cut to: Sloane/Slade writhing in pleasure as....

"Whoa," said Mitch, my sometime lover, who was visiting from the large city where he lived, "did you ever do that?"

"What? You mean the oral sex double-combo. Supersize it. No, have you?"

Mitch laughed. That's one thing I like about him, that he always gets my jokes. I like his brains too. He's an even better Scrabble player than I am, and does the Sunday *Times* crossword puzzle in ink. And I like the way he looks, tall and broad shouldered, with a pepper and salt mustache and an adorable lopsided smile. In fact, I like pretty much everything about Mitch, except for one thing: his ex-wife. Or rather the fact that she isn't "ex." Technically. Exactly.

I've known Mitch Connelly since law school, when we sat together in Civil Procedure class and shared notes on Federal Court jurisdiction. We were attracted even then, but I was married and he wasn't; and then I wasn't married and he was; and then he wasn't and I was again. Then we lost touch. Then I met him at a bar conference seven years ago, and he was separated and I was divorced, and after a couple of margaritas we found ourselves in bed, making up for lost time. And then he got unseparated again, which is to say, on-again. Now he's off-again. "You realize, of course, you have no future with this man," Janet reminds me every time Mitch visits. Which may very well be part of his appeal, though I hesitate to admit this, even to Janet.

"I meant did you stuff tissues in your top when you were 16?" he said.

No. But I did own one of those padded jobs that made you look as if you'd had two ice cream cones sutured to your torso.

God help us, Mitch groaned.

Easy for him to say. How could a man possibly understand?

Beautiful breasts can change a woman's life.

Cut to: "Nola": "I used to be that shy girl sitting in the corner who nobody paid attention to. Now I have the confidence that comes with knowing that whenever I walk into a room, all the men will be thinking, 'Hey, great tatas.'"

Cut to: "Cherie," shot only from the neck down: "I used to spend an hour every day putting on makeup. But now that guys talk only to my chest, I no longer bother with cosmetics, and I can use that time to work out at the gym. I'm in the best shape I've been in years."

Cut to:"Bree": "It is such a relief not to have to worry ever again that the first time I get naked with somebody, he'll say:

Cut to: Sloane/Slade at orgy:

"You got a nice ass, but your tits are too small."

When Attorney Stern had asked Tiffany Reed if Tiffany would like to appear in a short film exposing Dr. Sloane, Tiffany said sure, even though it would mean Tiffany would have to show the whole world the humongous boobs with the nips pointing in opposite directions, which she never showed anybody but Craig. Of course they'd cover her face with a blue dot, the hot Latino dude had said, and disguise her voice, but still...some girls in Tiffany's position might have hesitated to turn themselves into a national freak show, even for a good cause. Of course, those other girls might not have had Tiffany's creative side, or her respect for everything "artistic."

Sloane/Slade: "You got a nice ass but your tits are too small ..."

Sloane: Here at the Centers for Aesthetic Enhancement, we not only can change your appearance, we can change your life.

Cut to: bare-breasted Tiffany Reed, face obscured by blue dot: "How did Sloane change my life? I'll tell you how. He made me like a (bleeping) freak, that (bleeping) pervert."

"See ever since I'd had any boobs at all I wanted bigger ones, but not like stripper big; not like a total slut big..."

"Brilliant, Esposito is fucking brilliant," Tiffany passed Craig the nachos. "Didn't I tell you?"

Craig grimaced. He'd had about enough of fucking brilliant Esposito.

"You spent half a fucking day with the dude, and he cuts your part down to, like, five fucking minutes? I don't call that so fucking brilliant."

Tiffany gave Craig a look of pity at his fundamental incomprehension of the creative process, (which might explain, she thought, why *Scrambled Brains* was still playing late night gigs in pizza joints).

"It's all about the fucking editing ," she said. "Art is about the fucking editing."

Epilogue

—Although what became known as the "pornomercial" aired late at night in only ten cities, news of it quickly spread on the internet. Soon it began showing up on public access channels everywhere; then on the foreign language stations, dubbed in Spanish and Korean. Women from four states came forward to tell their own stories about Dr. Sloane, and Sloane was defrocked or desmocked or whatever it is they do to wayward physicians. And then a prosecutor got interested in the allegations of a certain 16-year old who traded sex for liposuction, and Sloane got put away for a very long time. Sloane's malpractice insurer quickly settled the three dozen lawsuits filed against Sloane, including Tiffany's. Sloane's Ferrari was seized by creditors.

—Tiffany used the money from the settlement to get a breast reduction operation and to enroll in the Hospitality Management program at the University of Las Vegas, where she is an A student. She and Craig have bought a house in the Vegas suburbs, and plan to marry soon. Craig's band has just produced its first CD, "Over Hard."

—Ramon's role as director, cinematographer and general

artistic visionary of "Be Everything You Can Be" became well-known in the underground film community. While at one time he'd dreamed of making it big in Hollywood, he now thought there was more integrity in being an elusive cult figure whose enigmatic short subjects, including the prize-winning *Fridgedario*, draw crowds for midnight showings in college towns everywhere.

He describes his current project, *Sub-Zero,* as an homage to his adopted land, the designer appliance serving as a metaphor for America in all its gorgeous abundance and stainless steel industrial glitter. But it can be a cold, cold country too, he says, especially for an immigrant.

Melissa Crane stared at me.

"You mean to say BGFH was actually just the four of you?"

There had been much speculation about the identity of BGFH, the mysterious production company behind the ad.

"Bratty Guys From Harvard," insisted one conservative talk-show host, noting the puerile, sophomoric content.

Disgruntled copywriters ironically subverting the infomercial form, said the professor of contemporary culture at Rutgers.

"And what did it actually stand for?" Melissa Crane asked. "Everybody wondered."

"BGFH? Ah yes—Book Group from Hell. Our little private joke."

"And you mean to tell me you never told, and no one ever suspected?"

"No. We were invisible women, and we meant to keep it that way.

Our invisibility was what we had going for us. It was our superpower, you might say. Fortunately, the last thing anyone would suspect was that the ad might be an example of menopausal zest at its zestiest. No one thinks that way, not in our society."

Well, hardly anyone…

Which brings me to the painful subject of Jason Wolf, damn him.

I flipped over the grimy card the young man—boy really—had shoved at me. "Jason Wolf," it read, "Investigative Journalist, the *Afternoon Gazette*."

More like Cub Reporter, I thought. I wondered if there still was such a thing as a cub reporter, or if the breed went out with Jimmy Olsen of the *Daily Planet,* to be replaced by unpaid interns.

Jason sort of resembled Jimmy Olsen, in fact, with his pale freckled skin, kinky red hair parted to the side, and expression of bedrock innocence that made his stabs at sophistication seem touching and faintly ridiculous.

"Jason Wolf?" I repeated. The name sounded vaguely familiar.

"Tiffany may have mentioned me?"

Oh right. Tiffany had talked about going to the "press," specifically Craig's cousin Jason, who had just gotten his first job out of journalism school, and was eager to sink his teeth into something a little sexier than Planning Commission meetings.

She never did contact Jason as far as I knew, and I'd forgotten all about him until he showed up unannounced at my office, begging Sylvia the receptionist for just five minutes of my valuable time.

As it happened, I was going through a slow patch just then, and had spent most of the afternoon, feet on desk, trying to make a dent in my eight-month backlog of *New Yorker* magazines. Jason Wolf might not be a paying client, but at least he was a momentary distraction from cartoons that made me feel stupid.

"Excuse me, but could I have that back now?" Jason pointed at the card. "It's my last one."

"You want it *back*?"

"Ad revenues are down, at least that's what they tell me. They had to economize someplace."

He opened his hazel eyes wide, in mute appeal.

"I told them it makes a poor first impression."

"That's OK. Don't worry about it."

Jason Wolf collapsed gratefully into the client chair, and flipped open a brand new notebook.

"I'll only take a few minutes of your time. I know you must be a very busy person." He pointed to my cluttered desk.

"Right," I said, discreetly shoving the Fiction double issue beneath a pile of unread deposition transcripts. "So how can I help you, Mr. Wolf?"

He didn't answer immediately. Instead he drummed a chewed pencil against his forehead, jiggled his knee, gulped air as if he were drowning, and finally blurted:

"It's about Dr. Sloane, actually. About that ad, the one with him performing the—er—acts—you've heard about it?"

"Anyone who hasn't been living in a cave for the last six weeks has heard about it. So?"

"So I thought you might have some idea how Tiffany's post-operative photos got into the filmmaker's hands. She says she gave them to you."

"Excuse me? You're saying you saw them?"

He blushed.

"Oh, not the—uh—things themselves. The pictures. Craig showed me the pictures once. Nipples pointing in opposite directions. Not something you see every day. You don't forget it. At least not if you're a trained journalist, you don't. And when the pictures turned up in the ad, I asked myself, how did they get there, and I find out you had a copy."

"I *had* a copy, Jason. Past tense. I gave mine back to Tiffany months ago."

True, strictly speaking. I didn't mention that I'd given another copy to Ramon, who had used the photographs as part of the closing montage, *Boobs Gone Wrong.*

"You're sure?"

"Of course I'm sure. Now if there isn't anything else, I'm a busy…"

He nibbled his index finger.

"Just one more thing..."

I tensed. He had to know *something*, or what was he doing here?

He pointed at the card, lying on my desk.

"It's...you forgot to give it back."

I tucked the card into his shirt pocket, and waved him out the door. I couldn't help liking the kid. But I also couldn't help having an uneasy feeling about him.

I suspected even then, I guess, that I had not heard the last of Jason Wolf, investigative journalist.

Melissa Crane's large dark eyes opened wide. She really was a very pretty girl, smart too. She deserved better than her current romantic catastrophe, an androgynous musician named Neville, who wore narrow three-piece black suits, and weighed less than she did. Did I think it was weird, she had asked me, him wanting her to dress up as a praying mantis?

Melissa Crane had started to confide in me, I'm not sure why. But I found myself enjoying the experience; welcoming the opportunity to pass on my hard-earned female wisdom.

"Generally speaking," I said, "I've found it's a good idea to avoid men who equate sex with death."

Melissa Crane was beginning to become like the daughter I was beginning to be a little relieved I'd never had.

She nodded as if she understood, and quickly changed the subject.

"So you knew Jason Wolf even before the kidnapping?"

"Oh yes. He had been tracking us for some time by then, though we didn't realize it, of course."

"Well," she began, much too casually… "as long as we're on the subject of the kidnapping anyway,.."

She activated the machine.

There it was at last—the kidnapping. I knew it would only be a matter of time before she got around to the kidnapping, even though she had claimed, in her letter to me, that she was a serious scholar, looking to link us to the long tradition of woman warriors going back to Queen Boadicea of Britain. I never would have agreed to cooperate with what she'd called her "research" otherwise. Half the cheesy journalists in America had been after us to talk about the kidnapping, ever since Jason Wolf had written that piece in the "Times" greatly exaggerating our role. We'd turned them all down, needless to say. We had no interest in becoming a public spectacle. Just the opposite.

"You need to understand everything from the beginning, or what are we doing here?" I cut her short. "We were about so much more than the kidnapping. And I want to go back and tell you about Carole, and how it started for her, with a small act of defiance involving her odious boss Bill Washington, the head of County operations at the time…"

Book Two
Carole

Chapter Four

Carole Goes to the Office

Carole Hansen was doing what she usually did at Bill Washington's so-called "management" meetings. She daydreamed, or planned her next vacation, or wondered whether she should tactfully raise the subject of Viagra with her husband Henry. Early in her long civil service career, Carole had mastered the good bureaucrat's art of pretending to pay rapt attention, while actually compiling next month's grocery list. Multi-tasking, she called it.

But now that she had reached the very top of the civil service ladder, a perch from which she could only be dislodged for embezzling public funds, or being found in bed with a 15-year-old, she barely bothered even pretending anymore. Instead, she scribbled revenge fantasies in her scratch pad as Washington, the Chief of County Operations, droned on about his latest idiot pet project, something to do with making jail inmates earn their keep by renting them out to telemarketing firms.

Washington had been talking for half-an-hour straight. She'd clocked him, the hypocrite, he who put a five minute lid on everyone else's air time, but none, of course, on his own; clocked him by his precious Rolex watch which he'd displayed on the conference table in front of him, so he could tap it in the middle of whatever you were saying, and announce, "Sorry, time's up," though really he wasn't sorry at all. She wished she hadn't arrived late and gotten stuck with the wobbly, narrow-backed secretary's chair right next to his. She squirmed on the insufficiently padded seat, turning her head to blunt the impact of his lime-scented cologne.

Still, it can't possibly last much longer, she thought, meaning not only his blather, but his tenure in the top job. It went in cycles, she knew, this business of putting a real hard-ass in charge. There would be some minor scandal involving, say, paving contracts, and the County Council would rush to hire the meanest SOB it could find—preferably someone whose résumé included the word "warden"—and instruct him to whip things into shape. This worked about as well as might be expected, which is to say things went on exactly as they always had, only now people were forced to become much more devious about taking every Wednesday afternoon off to play golf. The predictable resentments festered; the predictable backstabbing machinations occurred, and Whip-into-Shape was soon dumped in favor of Conciliator-Who-Can-Bring-Us-Together, whose résumé usually included the words "therapeutic modalities."

But Washington was the hardest of the many hard-asses Carole had seen pass through during her 25 years of public employment. Your typical hard-ass, in her experience, quickly gave up any naive notions of reforming the bureaucracy, and contented himself with talking tough, while leaving the difficult business of running municipal services to those who knew how—herself, for instance, or her good friend Dennis Melnick over in Planning, or a few other Lifers everybody respected.

Washington was a different kind of hard-ass. He enjoyed messing with people's heads. He would summon some low-level clerk, some timid older woman just marking time until retirement, and demand that she justify herself. His victim, who'd never had to consider the question before, would stammer something about data entry or file maintenance. What data, Washington would probe. And how do you enter it? He would give her exactly five minutes to answer, as timed by The Watch. Washington was determined to break her down, make her confess that she could be replaced by voice recognition software at a fraction of the cost. In five minutes with Washington she would lose every speck of self-esteem she'd gained under the three-year reign of the last Conciliator-Who-Brought-Us-Together.

An odious man, Carole thought. Good word—odious. She rolled it around on her tongue, murmuring. Oh-dee-us. Or with a Canadian accent: ow-dee-us. Ow-dee-oos.

"You had something to contribute here Carole?" Washington's voice roused her from her reverie.

She looked up.

"I was just imagining the conversation," she drawled. " Hi Ma'am, this is Duane over in Cellblock B, wondering if I could interest you in some vinyl windows today."

Washington looked murder at her. She knew what he was thinking. Every time Carole opened her mouth, she subverted his authority.

It's not that she objected to authority, as such. She knew, from her reading on the subject, that we are a hierarchical species; that consequently, whenever we gather, individuals strive to establish relative status, and that this is especially true when there are insecure blowhards present, such as Bill Washington. She didn't even mind that many of the authority figures she came across seemed to have the IQ of the average eggplant. Rising to the top had nothing to do with brains, she reminded herself. It had to do with the urge towards power, and being willing to kiss a lot of backsides in the service of that urge. And luck, of course. It also had a lot to do with luck.

No, it wasn't authority itself she minded, but the abuse of authority—the way Washington bullied Dennis, for instance, as he was doing right now. This was Bill's way of reasserting dominance, she figured, after her challenge to his supremacy. Consider the revealing body language: Washington's over-developed arms clasped behind his pink wrestler's neck; the chunky thighs spread to suggest the outline of his genitalia. Like the silverback gorilla making himself appear larger to intimidate lower-ranked males.

"Melnick—this report on drug enforcement policy is a total piece of shit."

Subtle as a gorilla too.

Dennis cowered inside his cheap suit and bent his head. Submitting. He was beginning to develop a bald spot on his crown, she noticed, and this touched her, the light fuzz there like a baby's. Poor Dennis, the kind of competent, decent, under-appreciated man who is the backbone of any organization; the one you could always count on to grind out a 50-page last-minute budget analysis for some indifferent councilmember, who'd promptly toss the whole thing into the garbage pail. Dennis would just shrug. What could you do?

It made Carole angry sometimes, the way Dennis refused

to stick up for himself. What did he have to lose? They could no more fire Dennis than they could fire Carole. But this wasn't Dennis' way, she realized. He'd been knuckling under to bullies all his life, from that very first relinquishment of his lunch money in kindergarten, and by now it was a tough habit to break.

A shame, Carole thought, because in other respects she liked Dennis very much, admired him even. He read good books and enjoyed talking about them. (She couldn't remember the last time she'd caught Henry reading a book, much less discussing one.) He played tournament level chess. He cared passionately about the natural world, leading walks for the Audubon Society; passing around petitions to save endangered species…

Washington fastened on his prey, blue pig eyes glittering.

"That no-jail-time/diversion-for-treatment bullshit has been tried everywhere, and it never works Melnick. Never. Never. Never." And for good measure, "N-E-V-E-R!"

As if Washington knew anything about drug treatment programs. As if Washington knew anything about anything. She and Dennis joked about it—how Washington was always taking these "fact-finding" trips at taxpayer expense, but the only fact he ever seemed to find was where to go marlin fishing or get good sushi. In Hawaii or Florida, that is. If there were facts to be found in places like Detroit, he sent Dennis.

Dennis bobbed his small chin forward.

"After all, Bill," he said, "70% of American adults have tried it..."

Washington sneered. He had a long loose mouth, like a fish. He tapped The Watch, implying that Dennis was wasting

Washington's valuable time.

"It's still a crime, Melnick. An illegal crime. So maybe instead of this diversion crap, we should be thinking about more effective ways to implement Councilwoman Pirelli's Seek and Destroy initiative. That's our real mandate here."

Carole groaned. A few of the others rolled their eyes when they thought Washington wasn't looking.

Susanna Pirelli's brainchild, "Seek and Destroy" was supposed to monitor suspicious surges in electrical usage to detect marijuana home-grow operations. Never mind the invasion of privacy; never mind those embarrassing busts of senior citizens running extra loads of laundry, Washington never missed an opportunity to promote the fiasco.

Carole wondered if it was true, the rumor that Washington and Pirelli were sleeping together. She found the image comically repulsive—Washington's flounder mouth on Pirelli's unpleasant little chihuahua face. Yet it was hard to explain how else Washington could have gotten his job after what was described as a "national search," and Pirelli had been head of the hiring committee…

She jotted a note in her scratchpad.

Hire detective? Catch Washington and Pirelli in the act? Send photos to P's jealous husband Guido?

No, she'd never do it, but it was fun to think about sitting here, bored to death.

She remembered the look on Sandi's face after Sandi had tossed that cellphone in the fish tank. The thrill of transgression, Sandi had called it on the way home, and then reminisced about all her other thrilling transgressions, most of them over thirty years in the past by now, but still, it had made Carole feel so—

dowdy—in retrospect. So square-jawed, big-boned, and stolid. Carole had married Henry, an electrical engineer, straight out of college, and had three children boom-boom-boom, while people like Sandi were dropping acid and frolicking naked in campus fountains and plotting to overthrow the State. Carole sometimes wished she too had a misspent youth to get all nostalgic about every time they played "Come the Revolution" on the Oldies station.

Too late now.

Washington seemed to be winding down at last, preparing to adjourn, but not before taking one final swipe at Dennis, who was supposed to go on a long-planned eco-vacation to Costa Rica in two days to observe tropical wildlife in the forest canopy.

"Oh, and Melnick, I'll need a complete redraft by the end of the week."

That would leave Dennis a good half-hour to get ready for his trip, Carole figured. That is, if he cut out the non-essentials, such as sleeping and eating.

Dennis wiped his hand over his thinning hair, causing a few desolate flakes to float down to his bowed shoulders. It just about broke Carole's heart.

Kidnap Washington and hogtie him. Give him exactly five minutes to justify his life.

Washington turned his head away, searching for a fresh victim, and the next thing Carole knew a certain Rolex watch somehow found itself on the floor, and a certain wobbly chair somehow rolled right over it, with a gratifying crunch, like the sound of a large beetle being flattened underfoot.

It happened so quickly nobody even noticed at first. Nobody but Dennis, whose Bassett hound eyes stared in astonished wonder, as though he'd spotted some Tasmanian woodthrush blown by perverse winds into the wrong hemisphere. Then he smiled—a warm, intelligent smile that made him almost attractive.

Washington turned around, spotted the remains of his watch, screamed *fuckohfuck*. And when the others followed his eyes to the shards of expensive metal and glass sprayed over the grey carpet, a tremor seemed to pass through the crowd, an imperceptible quiver of pure happiness. Near the back of the room, a senior finance analyst high-fived the head of Human Resources, while the Chief Engineer elbowed the ribs of the Mass Transit guy (though ordinarily they disliked each other, and were barely on speaking terms). And way over in a corner, John McDougal, the Jail Superintendent, a man so gloomy he'd been nicknamed "Jack the Mortician," was seen, for the first and last time, to laugh.

They began gathering up their papers then, preparing to leave; to settle into their cubicles for another day of quietly ensuring that the sewers got pumped and the grass got mowed and the cops got paid and the permits got stamped and the fires got quenched and that, in general, life went on as it always had. And Carole thought that it was a fine, an honorable thing to do, and there were worse ways a person could spend her one and only passage through this vale of tears.

Better ways too.

Plant dope in Washington's garage? Call in tip? Rig wiring to show electrical surge. Ask Henry how.

"Bill Washington?" Melissa Crane frowned. "Why does that name sound so familiar?"

"Well, it's a familiar sounding name. But you probably remember him in connection with the Clyde Arbuckle business. It was all over the papers and on TV a couple of years ago."

"Clyde Arbuckle, the developer? You don't mean to tell me you had a hand in that one too?"

"Oh, it was mostly Carole and her friend Dennis, though we each had our parts to play. And in this case luck, or should I say Clyde Arbuckle's bad luck, also played a part. But even then, it might never have happened if Dennis Melnick hadn't been out watching birds at Robinson's Marsh that day…"

Chapter Five
Swamp Creatures

Dennis Melnick wiped his glasses and peered again at the Black Rail through his new $1600 Swarovski birding scope, the one his ex-wife Rowena had called the last straw, proof positive that he loved his stupid birds more than he loved her. Which was true. Maybe he never had loved her, not even at the beginning. He wasn't sure what Love was exactly, but he suspected it was something more than the vague gratitude and dim lust he'd felt for her in the early days, and which he'd called Love because she'd insisted on it. "Do you love me," she'd demanded when she proposed to him on their twenty-third date. By that time, he'd gotten used to seeing her every Saturday night, and to the regular satisfaction of his never vigorous sexual needs. So he said, " I guess so." He'd forgotten to ask if she loved him. He doubted it.

This whole business of perpetuating the species was so much more straightforward for birds, he thought. A male, say, wishing to mate, might display his inflamed crest to the receptive female, who would signal her favor by plucking out his tail feather. Then he would mount her, eventually leading to eggs, brooding, chicks, and the next generation of adults in an eternal cycle Dennis found deeply satisfying in its animal simplicity.

It was Rowena's eggs, in fact, or rather her dwindling supply of viable eggs, that had prompted that abrupt proposal in the first place. She was 36 years old, she'd informed him, and her biological clock was ticking. She couldn't afford to wait around forever while Dennis got over his fear of commitment, or whatever his problem was.

So he'd married her, mainly because she was the only person who'd ever asked. It was hard now, five years later, to remember what the attraction had been. She was not an especially good-looking woman, that might have been part of it. He was shy around women in general, but pretty women he found absolutely terrifying.

After she left, Dennis wrote a poem expressing this, inspired by their first meeting at an over-29ers networking event, a poem which he called:

SOME DISENCHANTED EVENING

I noticed you when you walked in
I thought that all in all
I'd never seen vapor
Or even wallpaper
So fade into a wall.
We've a lot in common thought I
And the thought set my palms perspiring
As I lost myself admiring:
Your stringy hair
Your pasty skin
Your unengaging smile
The spinach beneath
Your two front teeth
Your total lack of style.

How unadorned she is, I thought
Approachable and plain.
And I knew such a chance
For a great romance
Would not soon come again...

He'd sent it to her with a belated Valentine's Day card, and a box of stale half-price candy he hoped she choked on. It was the first truly cruel thing he'd ever done, and it had felt surprisingly...good. Carole was right. His problem was that he was too nice, and it made people—people like Rowena, like Bill Washington—want to step all over him.

But he'd come here to Robinson's Marsh to forget about all that: about love; about Rowena; about Washington's ever-increasing demands on Dennis' time, for projects of ever-increasing stupidity.

He watched the Rail sidlc towards its distinctive dome-shaped, canopied nest. Remarkable birds, able to slip through a marsh without disturbing a single reed, hence the name "Rail," as in thin as a.... He'd been surprised to see a Black Rail here in a wetland so close to an urban area, especially a nesting rail. But then, he often was happily surprised at what he found in Robinson's Marsh; multitudes of wrens; that rare yellow-headed blackbird once.

And even on a perfectly ordinary day, you could count on spotting some perfectly ordinary marvel, a Great blue heron maybe. They were common hereabouts, and heart-stoppingly beautiful both in stillness and in flight—like the one he saw that time he'd taken Carole to the marsh, just after he'd bought the scope with his tax refund.

Let's spend the refund on a discount cruise to Acapulco, Rowena had insisted, pulling out a brochure she claimed she just happened to pick up at a travel agency she just happened to be passing by on her way home from work. He understood at that moment the true awfulness of what he'd done in marrying her; maybe the true awfulness of marriage itself: to be so dismally…linked; to be obligated to share your house, your sleep, your evenings, even your tax refund with a person with whom you have not a single taste or inclination in common—a person like Rowena, so ill at ease with silence she read road signs aloud when they took car trips: Springfield, 40 miles. Icy when wet. Entering apple maggot quarantine area. He would find himself spasmodically clutching the wheel, as though he were throttling Rowena by proxy; anything to stop the incessant din of "Premium shopping outlets, next right," and, "This highway adopted by the Marblemount Kiwanis Club." Then he would stop the car and throw up on the side of the road. Passive-aggressive, Rowena called him. But the problem was that he was too plain *nice*, as Carole said.

Carole. He smiled, remembering the day he'd taken her to the marsh. He'd worn the red and black plaid flannel shirt she'd once complimented him on. "If you opened the top button," she had said, "it would make you look almost rugged." And that day at the marsh, he had.

They rarely saw each other outside work, so he'd been pleased when she said she'd grown interested in what she'd called "birdwatching." Birding, he'd told her. Nobody called it birdwatching any more—at least nobody who actually watched birds.

He could no longer see the rail, hidden now among the

reeds. He trained the scope instead on the far side of the marsh, where just last week he'd spotted an especially fine American bittern. It was gone—no surprise there—but he saw something else, something disagreeable even when seen across the length of the Council chambers, and truly horrifying viewed up close through the peerless optics of a Swarovski instrument. He saw the unlovely face of Councilwoman Sue Pirelli herself—short on chin, long on forehead, and with those protuberant green eyes suggestive of some hidden disease process, some hyperthyroidism of the spirit.

And she wasn't alone. A fat arm was draped across her shoulder; a hairy knuckle skimmed one of her tiny breasts; something vaguely reptilian licked her ropy neck.

It was the snaky tongue of none other than Clyde Arbuckle, developer of the infamous Arbuckle Villages. Arbuckle Pillages, their opponents called them, mammoth executive homes devouring farmland and open spaces the way Arbuckle now seemed to be devouring Pirelli's ear.

Though Dennis Melnick was not a man much given to wild (or even tame) flights of fancy, he had a dreadful vision as he stood there watching them. He saw his beloved marsh transformed into a huddle of 5000-square-foot fake-Tudor monstrosities, each with matching BMWs in the three-car garage and non-native shrubs in its minuscule front yard. Where the rail guarded its remarkable nest would be the security gate, with the sign: "Welcome to Wildwood Vista—real country living only minutes from the city."

A scream began to rise in him, an awful scream, like in that woodcut Carole had hanging over her desk, a scream all mouth and eyes and crazy sworls, like the fingerprints of your own personal demons.

And Dennis, a man who revered DNA in all its forms; a card-carrying member of the American Tarantula Society; the one who at summer barbecues always was sticking up for the right of the mosquito to express its mosquitoness, pointed the scope at the amorous pair and said, Bang, Bang, you're dead. It was the first truly homicidal impulse he'd ever had, and it had felt surprisingly...good.

Sometimes it would happen when she least expected it, like today in the department store where she'd gone at lunch hour to buy Henry a robe for Father's Day. She'd spot a somehow familiar gray-haired, stoop-shouldered woman across the aisle, an ordinary woman, in need of a haircut and some lipstick.

And she'd realize, with a shock, that the woman was her own self, reflected in a pitiless full-length mirror looming up where it had no business to loom, in Men's Furnishings, of all places.

It disturbed and depressed her for the rest of the day. Not that she's vain. Rawboned, ruddy-faced women had no business being vain, she'd decided early on. Vanity, in her case, could lead only to heartbreak. And she'd never seen the point to heartbreak, except perhaps as an engine for moving a plot forward.

Lives are not plots (something else Carole had realized early on), which was one reason she'd married Henry, a man you could count on never to provide a nasty surprise denouement; a comfortable man, a good father and handy around the house. And if he seemed to grow duller and more silent every year; if he now spent most of his spare time in his workshop building yet another unnecessary bookcase for the grandchildren they didn't have yet, well, she'd gotten what she'd bargained for, hadn't she? And only once in a while did she allow herself to wonder if she'd gotten what she wanted. Or if she even knew what that was.

No, she wasn't vain, but still it had been a disappointment to see herself looking so...old in that uncompromising reflection. She reminded herself, sensibly, that human females are genetically programmed to self-destruct around age 50, when their breeding years are over; that what was happening to her was the end product of a hundred million years or so of mammalian evolution. Nothing to feel bad about. And yet bad was exactly how she'd felt.

Back at the office, she picked up the file Dennis had dropped on her desk that morning, with the post-it note on the top: "Must talk immediately!! Important!! Robinson's Marsh. Orange-spotted Western newt. May be Endangered! Down to last five mating pair!"

She sighed. Carole could barely keep up with all the *human* misery she was supposed to feel guilty about. And here was Dennis, always going on about some dung beetle losing ground to the encroaching Las Vegas suburbs; or a bat in Paraguay hunted nearly to extinction by ignorant villagers who ground up the bones to make a love potion.

What did he expect her to do about it anyway—take out a personals ad in *National Geographic*?

"Woolly bat seeks same; Me: 8 1/4 inches, Height, weight proportional; enjoy hanging upside down, moonlight rambles, and the smell of fresh guano."

Robinson's Marsh.

Dennis had taken her there for her first lesson in bird-watching. Birding they called it now, he'd said, which certainly sounded more masculine and assertive. But she preferred the older word, and the appealing images it conjured of thick knees below baggy Bermuda shorts; of earnest, elderly maiden ladies in men's trousers, sitting in their parlors, comparing their life lists, their serene days not overly cluttered with the mess of human connection.

Who knows but that she might have become just such a bird-counting maiden lady, if in her senior year in college, she hadn't gotten that flat tire on her way to physics class, and Henry hadn't stopped to fix it; or if she hadn't been so impressed by his quiet competence; his manly (as it seemed to her then) ease with the material world.

THE ROAD NOT TAKEN, she scrawled on a notepad, underlining the words three times with slashes of magic marker. But that wasn't it exactly. She didn't feel as if she'd *taken* any road at all. It was more like she'd just wound up someplace in error. As if, due to a cock-up in cosmic bookkeeping, she'd been allotted the wrong life, while her real life—the life in which she had a studio in Paris and smoked Gauloises and took much younger lovers—rolled merrily along without her in some parallel reality.

A stray nail on the freeway, and everything changes forever. So how could any thinking person not believe in a Universe governed by chance? She tried to find the idea comforting. Randomness wasn't such a terrible thing for the Universe to be governed by, when one considered the alternatives—the whim of wrathful Jehovah, for instance, or similar disagreeable gods.

Robinson's Marsh.

It had been so lovely—all cattails and sudden eruptions of red-winged blackbirds.

And Dennis, who seemed clumsy and awkward at the office, had moved with surprising grace through the swaying reeds. He looked better too, shed of his ill-fitting cheap suits, with the trousers that ended before his shoes began. She had mentioned it to him once, tactfully she hoped, that he might have better luck with women if he weren't always flashing an inch or so of white cotton sock. It was just such tiny things, she knew, that could doom a relationship before it even started.

But that day at the marsh he'd worn blue jeans, nicely faded and just snug enough to show off an unexpectedly tempting rear-end, and well-muscled thighs. Carole had always realized in an abstract way that Dennis had a body, but she'd never been aware of it as an actual, corporeal fact before. She'd made a mental note: mention to him that if he went to one of those over-40 singles events, he should wear the jeans, and that flannel shirt, and the fisherman's hat that covered his bald spot and brought out the russet tone of his eyes.

Then, that amazing heron—viewed through the scope it was like some gorgeous Persian miniature come to life, bobbing a delicate, enameled path through the softly parting grasses. The sight of it made her shiver, the way pictures of far-off galaxies sometimes made her shiver, or Beethoven's Late Quartets. She and Dennis had smiled at each other, wordlessly sharing a brief experience of the ineffable. This had never happened to her before with a man, and it troubled her a little. And she had to admit, thrilled her a little too.

Henry wasn't a person you shared experiences of the ineffable with, however brief. She couldn't fault him for this, not really. It wasn't the kind of thing you could cite as grounds for divorce after thirty years of trouble-free marriage. "And in conclusion your Honor, when we saw the Northern Lights on our cruise to Alaska, the best he could manage was, "quite a show huh?" Yet she knew it was just such tiny things that could doom a relationship....

The phone rang.

Dennis. A very upset Dennis.

And no wonder.

Clyde Arbuckle, it seemed, had just bought Robinson's Marsh.

Carole knew about Arbuckle, of course. The portly developer frequently appeared before the County Council seeking permits to construct what he called his vision for the future—an Arbucklean dystopia of hideous strip malls and great blue glass rectangles hermetically sealed to prevent the desperate drones inside from leaping to their deaths.

And in this, he could always count on Councilwoman Sue Pirelli's enthusiastic support, her unwavering commitment to always doing the wrong thing. The Councilwoman had no sentimental attachment to the unprofitable farmland and falling-down old heaps (architectural treasures) Arbuckle displaced. These she filed under 'L' for 'Losers', the same place she filed the homeless, the unemployed, the Third World, and most of the Democratic Party.

"I saw Arbuckle out there just yesterday, sticking his tongue in Sue Pirelli's ear," Dennis said.

"Are you telling me Arbuckle literally had his tongue inside her ear. You don't mean he was bending her ear?" Carole's heart beat faster. Physical—as opposed to metaphoric—tongue-to-ear contact, if it had occurred, and if it could be proved...well this wouldn't sit well with Pirelli's churchgoing constituents, not to mention with Pirelli's jealous husband, Guido.

"They were... fondling," Dennis chose his words carefully, recognizing the significance of what he said. "Definitely. I'd describe what they were doing as fondling."

Fondling, Carole thought, happily. Fondling implied something more than the normal affection one rapacious predator might show to another.

"I wondered when I saw them," Dennis went on, "why do it in Robinson's Marsh, of all places. Bugs. Prickly grass, no mini-bar..."

So Dennis had checked the Planning Commission records. And there it was—the permit request for Arbuckle City, a new concept in urban design to be constructed on the site of the soon-to-be-former Robinson's Marsh.

"He has to be stopped," Dennis said, "by any means necessary."

Which brought Dennis to the romantic troubles of the rare Orange-spotted Western newt.

Clyde Arbuckle was not feeling his usual delight just in being Clyde Arbuckle this morning.

And it was all because of Robinson's Marsh.

First the problem had been old man Robinson, and now this repulsive little salamander. Robinson would never consider selling his marsh, oh no, over his dead body. Not even when

Arbuckle had promised to name the development Robinson Woods, or Robinson Downs. Not even when Robinson was diagnosed with inoperable cancer—a time when most men would be giving serious thought to ensuring that their names lived after them—would Robinson entertain Arbuckle's generous proposal. On the contrary. Robinson had tried to change his will, practically with his dying breath, binding his heirs to maintain the property forever for the benefit of its unique wildlife. Fortunately, Robinson had slipped into a coma before Robinson's attorney, who happened to be a friend of Arbuckle's, could draw up the necessary paperwork.

Then Robinson's daughter Evelyn...whereas Robinson had been rigid and unyielding when it came to his principles, steely-eyed, prune-faced Evelyn was rigid and unyielding when it came to money. Once she'd detected his desire—oh he'd tried to hide it, but she had a nose for those things, the greed in her calling to the greed in him maybe—she had driven a hard bargain. So now Arbuckle had most of his cash tied up in this swamp—sorry—precious wetland. All the right wheels had been oiled, and the right palms greased, and everything in general nicely lubricated to smooth the way for what Arbuckle meant to be his crowning achievement: Arbuckle City, a revolutionary concept in urban design. When along comes this Orange-spotted newt, throwing what you might call a reptile in the ointment.

As nasty a creature as the good Lord in his wisdom had ever created, Arbuckle thought, staring at the rare specimen he'd bought illegally from a Florida outfit which specialized in such things; watching the little beast squirm blindly around the stark moonscape of its terrarium. Said to be nearly as poisonous as the Japanese blowfish; merely to lick its craggy skin (though Arbuckle couldn't imagine why anyone would be tempted) was to suffer agonizing pain; you bite it, or it bites you and you die unpleasantly within hours. Consequently, the newt had no natural enemies except the automobile, a certain garter snake, and now, Clyde Arbuckle.

Nevertheless, for reasons not clearly understood, the newt population was failing to thrive. Mating problems, the County biologist said. Arbuckle studied his new pet. If he looked like that, he'd have mating problems too.

He pressed his squat nose against the glass.

"Prepare for doom," he hissed. But he knew it wasn't that simple.

Now if ever Arbuckle had seen a species that richly deserved extinction, this was it. Unfortunately, the law, in its infinite stupidity, might view the matter differently, or so Arbuckle's attorneys advised. Since Robinson's Marsh was the newt's principal remaining habitat, there might have to be an environmental-impact this, or a wetland-preservation-study that, all delaying construction, and costing Arbuckle interest he really couldn't afford, not in this uncertain economic climate.

Pirelli had assured him that she was working on it, that it all would turn out right in the end, and that the end would come sooner, rather than later. He hoped so. He was getting really tired of banging her, the skinny, demanding twat. She wasn't his type, first off. Twenty years too old, twenty pounds too scrawny, no tits to speak of....

But that wasn't the main problem. He'd banged plenty of women who weren't his type, before he'd gotten rich enough to be picky. When he'd been just plain "Fat Clyde" or "Porko," he didn't even realize he had a type. He'd been grateful for whatever he could get. It was only after he'd made his fortune, and his name was on half the buildings in town, that he became "Big Daddy Clyde" to the unlimited supply of models, exotic dancers, aspiring actresses etc. who suddenly found him irresistibly attractive. Sure, he realized they were only after his money, but that didn't bother him. The way Clyde saw it, what was the point of becoming rich and important if you still had to go to all the trouble of getting people to love you for yourself?

So he wouldn't have minded banging Pirelli, even though she wasn't his type, except that the whole thing was so humiliating. And not humiliating in a good-dirty-fun-handcuffs-to-the-bedpost kind of way either.

"It isn't about the sex for her," Bill Washington had confided to him one night, when they got drunk together, "it's about power."

This had been clear from that first time at the Red Horse Inn. She'd invited him to meet her there so they could discuss Arbuckle City, and he had brought along an envelope stuffed with cash, just in case. Maybe that's what gave her the idea. Or maybe she'd had it all along.

Their dinner conversation had been perfectly business-like, except for the casual remark she'd made when he heaped his baked potato with an entire cup of sour cream. "Eat up," she'd said. "It's a real turn on—the sight of a little bitty dick dangling like a worm under a gigantic gut." That should've been a warning sign to him right there.

Then she'd told him how excited she was about the concept of Arbuckle City, a radical experiment in urban design.

How she was prepared to call in a lot of favors to make it happen. It wouldn't be easy. He could expect serious opposition from the save-the-everything loonies of the Left. Arbuckle had nodded. Said he understood. That he appreciated her help and support and that if there was anything he could do for her...

Then he'd placed the envelope on the table between them. She looked around. Maybe we should continue this conversation in my room, she said. He'd been surprised that she had a room since the Red Horse was only 45 minutes from the city, but certainly he understood the need for discretion.

Once inside the room she didn't waste much time. She tore off her cashmere dress, and slipped out of the lacy black underpants.

"Make love to me," she ordered, pushing him back on to the flower-patterned bedspread, and straddling his huge belly. And he'd done his best, considering he wasn't the least bit attracted to the lady, plus he'd just eaten a five-thousand calorie meal containing an entire week's saturated fat allowance. It didn't help to look at her either, so he just closed his eyes and thought of Arbuckle City as it might be: its gleaming towers, its pedestrian malls, its gracious town homes. He grunted with pleasure.

"I'm glad it's good for you," she barked. "Now if you could just manage to get it up, it might be good for me too."

She slid off him, and squeezed his cock hard, as if she were popping a party favor. Ouch!

"The next time I decide to climb Mount Arbuckle," she said, unkindly, "you'd better bring along Viagra, and some bottled oxygen."

But that wasn't the really humiliating part. That came next.

He was pulling on his clothes, preparing to leave, when her bony forefinger tapped the night table.

"Aren't you forgetting something?"

He checked his pockets. Wallet. Cell phone. Sunglasses. Keys.

He shook his head.

"You didn't think I was giving it away for free did you, Big Boy?"

Her voice went all whiskey-low and throaty.

"Hand it over, limpdick."

It took him a minute to realize what she meant. Then, hardly believing what he was doing, he tossed the envelope with its 20 Ben Franklins onto the bed. So this was her game. Political whore. In every sense of the word.

Talk about a sick fantasy.

Two grand, Arbuckle thought bitterly. For that you could get a top girl from Escorts Unlimited for a whole weekend. And they took credit cards too. Fabulous sex, plus frequent-flyer miles.

Now Pirelli called him every couple of weeks inviting him to "party." He made excuses as often as he could, but the longer he went between parties, the slower the permit process for Arbuckle City seemed to become. And Pirelli was getting bolder and more careless, almost as though she wanted them to be caught. That day at the marsh, for instance, he was sure someone had been watching them. He only prayed that that someone hadn't been sent by Guido Pirelli, who, frankly, scared the shit out of Arbuckle.

The well-known orthopedic surgeon often accompanied his wife to political functions. Short, stocky, reputedly of Sicilian heritage, with a single menacing eyebrow, Guido had this unnerving way of repeating your name when he met you, as if he were committing it to memory for future purposes you'd rather not think about.

"My father and my grandfather broke bones for a living," Dr. Pirelli liked to joke, "I put them back together. God bless America." Only Arbuckle wasn't sure the doctor was joking. He wouldn't have been surprised if somewhere in Guido's office, maybe in a drawer marked "biohazards," Pirelli kept a secret Rolodex with the names of contract killers who worked cheap. Or at least the names of contract maimers.

So lately Arbuckle found himself uneasy in public, and careful always to face the door in restaurants.

And who knew how long this would go on. And all because of a fucking LIZARD.

Clyde Arbuckle shook himself. He hadn't gotten to be Clyde Arbuckle by letting obstacles stand in his way.

He watched the specimen slithering over the gravel. Prepare for doom, he said again, but this time he meant it.

They were down to the last five pair, the biologist's report said. That meant ten. Ten little salamanders standing in a line, one ate poison, then there were nine...

Clyde Arbuckle had an idea...

The clotted tape which held Howie Berkowitz' glasses together clung briefly to the bridge of his nose, and there was a tearing sound as he removed the spectacles, preparing to deliver the bad news. It was only common courtesy, he believed, to go bare-eyeball with your client during such moments.

"The thing is, I'd feel better about your long-term prospects if you had maybe a panda out there, or even a halfway-decent-looking butterfly. I'm no expert on the Endangered Species Act—I'm just saying, the fifth most poisonous reptile on earth is a tough sell. Fair or not, a lot of people will think, 'good riddance'."

Dennis Melnick shook his cupped fists as if each contained a small, though not necessarily harmless, snake.

"Damn it, Mr. Berkowitz, it's not about the survival of the cutest," he shouted.

Whoa!! Howie was beginning to regret he'd agreed to see this Melnick person in the first place, strictly as a favor to Sandi. "You owe me one," Sandi had informed him. (He always seemed to owe Sandi one, though he never could remember for what.) Funny, Howie thought. First impression of the guy was strictly "Prince of Dorkness." Yet Howie knew, from long experience, that any man could be capable of anything, if you hit him straight where his own particular lunacy lived.

"How long do you suppose we have?" Melnick glowered, and stood up. He seemed large, even mildly threatening, when he did this, though Howie figured Melnick for only about five foot ten, six inches shorter than Howie himself.

Howie shrunk into his chair, and put the glasses back on. He felt safer behind them, as if they were his own personal Gardol shield. Did anybody else remember the Gardol shield, he wondered, from that 1950's toothpaste ad? Gardol—the triple-strength invisible barrier that protected against decay and by implication, nuclear attack. How the fuck should Howie know how long Melnick had? He hated when a client tried to pin him into a corner like that. Then they blamed it on you when things didn't work out, no matter how many times you said, "probably" or "just a guess," or "sorry, but I don't happen to own a crystal ball." Howie had been in this business long enough to realize that, by and large, people heard not what you said, but what they wanted to hear.

He cleared his throat.

"A year; 18 months maybe, with your basic procedural delays. More if you can work up a public outcry." Howie stared at the photograph of the Orange-spotted newt." Which I very much doubt."

Melnick nodded, and said, with an unnerving calm:

"Well I guess if the law won't help me, I'll just have to find another way, outside the law."

Howie always got a little uneasy when clients told him that. He pictured arson; he pictured bullet-riddled bodies hopping around the floor like Mexican jumping beans. And it would all be Howie's fault, because he had too much integrity to offer people false hope. Sometimes he wondered whether it would be better to let your nut job find out five years down the road, after two trials and three unsuccessful appeals, that the law couldn't do anything for him, by which time he'd be too exhausted, dispirited, pummeled by the system to be a danger to anybody but himself…

OK. So he'd give Melnick hope. No skin off his nose, even if technically he might be violating some Canon of Professional Ethics or other, probably the one about how thou shalt not counsel criminal conduct. Howie remembered that gossip

Sandi had passed on—Pirelli and Arbuckle boffing each other out in the swamp. Maybe true. Maybe not. Whatever. Keep Melnick and the rest of them busy and out of trouble, tracking it down.

"On the other hand, Mr. Melnick," he said, studying his manicured nails, "you could always consider good old-fashioned blackmail."

There were a lot of things Ramon would rather have been doing on a beautiful summer night than sitting in the parking lot of a Comfort Inn, waiting. The same way he'd waited at the La Quinta and the Red Horse, two weeks ago, three weeks ago. He'd trailed the skinny woman there, the politician. And then, each time, the fat man had shown up, sure enough, the way they said he would. Ramon recognized him from his picture in the papers, though this man didn't appear like a man who was there for purposes of making secret love to a woman not his wife; he looked more like a man who was there for purposes of having his wisdom teeth extracted.

And Ramon didn't see the point. Yes, each time, the skinny woman went in. And each time, the fat man shuffled in ten minutes later. Each time he came out in an hour, got in his big Mercedes and sped off. Then she came out, licking her lips. But this proved nothing.

Because all Ramon could see from the parking lot was the main entrance, with its carpet of rubber matting. For all Ramon knew, the fat man and the skinny woman could be having dinner at the coffee shop. Ramon had eaten once at such an establishment, and this might well explain the look of dread on the fat man's face.

Bored. He was bored. He slapped himself to stay awake. The ladies were counting on him, and he owed them so much. Without them, he never would have made "Be Everything You Can Be," and never would have become a revered cult figure in underground cinema circles, and might have remained nothing but a dishwasher his whole life. Whereas now, he only took the occasional fill-in restaurant gig during the summers, when the campuses where he was revered shut down.

It wasn't gratitude alone that kept him here at his post, however, squeezed in the little Honda. The fact is, while he was most in love with Ellie, in a way he was a little in love with all of them: with Carole, her elegant hands, the touch of Red Indian in her cheekbones, her cool, sexy intelligence; with Sandi's wild smoke-colored hair and the amused, worldly-wise wrinkles around her eyes; and sweet little Janet, the dark pixie, her pretty ankles peeking out from under the long, swirling skirts she always wore.

So when they had asked him to do it as a special favor and as a public service, how could he refuse?

He put the lens cap back on the camera. It would be at least another half-hour before the fat man and the skinny lady finished up whatever it was they were doing in there, and meanwhile...

There was something on the radio about a dead lizard. A dead rare lizard. Ramon switched stations until he found some salsa music. Then he must've fallen asleep. And he seemed to be dreaming about a man and a woman having an argument, also about lizards. But when he woke up, the fat man and the skinny woman were right in front of him, and the fat man was yelling, and the skinny woman was laughing. The fat man drove away. But the skinny woman didn't get in her car. She returned to the hotel entrance, and another man joined her there. A good-looking muscular man, but with a peculiar mouth, a long loose mouth, like a fish. Ramon removed the lens cap and began filming.

There were things Clyde Arbuckle would much rather be doing on a beautiful summer night than sitting in a bog, attempting to lure an extremely poisonous and ill-tempered creature into a trap.

But after the disaster with Ernesto, Clyde had concluded that if he wanted the job done right, he had no choice but to do it himself. So here he was, hunkered down in the prickly grass, slapping at the ravenous mosquitoes, experiencing the much-overrated Nature first-hand. Why those enviro-nuts were always battling to preserve it was beyond him.

At this point, he'd happily have given up the whole idea of Arbuckle City, if only he hadn't been leveraged to his eyeballs. If Arbuckle City went south, his entire jerry–rigged financial empire, held together as it was by equal parts creative accounting and outright fraud, went along with it. Twenty years of cunning and deceit down the toilet.

Damn Ernesto and his damned trophies.

When Clyde had decided that it was time to arrange for the premature extinction of the Orange-spotted Western newt, he'd gone looking for an exterminator, but not the licensed and bonded type you found in the Yellow Pages, offering to take out bats, rats, skunks, squirrels, moles, voles, snakes, hornets, raccoons, bees, fleas, termites or spiders for a fee.

What Clyde needed was a pest-control outlaw.

He'd spotted Ernesto's ad in a *Soldier of Destiny* magazine, which Clyde had picked up at the barbershop. "Exotic game specialist. Always gets his beast. No species too rare. Satisfaction guaranteed." Clyde liked the sound of that "no species too rare." This Ernesto clearly wasn't a man who would sweat stuff like the possibility of a $10,000 fine, and a brief term of incarceration in a Federal penitentiary.

Clyde called the number—a Miami area code.

Now you wouldn't think it would be easy to affront the professional dignity of the kind of person who kidnaps baby gorillas for a living, but it seems that Clyde had.

"Let me get this straight," Ernesto rumbled, in a voice like shards of ice. "You want me to go to a swamp and hunt down a fucking...salamander?"

Ten salamanders actually. And Clyde would pay well.

"Ten fucking salamanders. Why don't you just go step on the fucking things. They're three fucking inches long."

Clyde controlled his temper, and although the question clearly was rhetorical, he replied with equal chill:

"It isn't that simple. It has to look like natural causes."

"Right. They're gonna fucking autopsy a fucking lizard."

"Forget it," Clyde said, disliking Ernesto more every minute. "I'll find somebody else." Though he had no idea how or where.

Then Clyde could sense the shift in power.

"No. No," the other man's voice thawed now, wheedling

almost. "I'd be happy to do it. It's just not my usual line of work."

Of course, Clyde thought. These were hard times. Ernesto needed the job. Needed it desperately. The first thing people were likely to cut back on in an economic downturn were poached elephant tusks.

After only the most minimal haggling on Ernesto's part, Clyde agreed to give him a try, on a strictly piecework basis, plus he'd have to take care of his own travel expenses.

They mustn't meet, Clyde said. Lately, Clyde was convinced he was being watched. Yesterday at the motel, he had had a bad feeling about it, and not only because of the unpleasantness of the task at hand. So rather than interview the hunter in person, Clyde gave Ernesto the details on the phone. Whack them one at a time. Leave the bodies where they would be found. Clyde would pay a bounty on each head, no questions asked. Or on each tail, he joked, feeling expansive, the way he always did when he had concluded a deal that was very much to his advantage.

Never joke with an idiot, Clyde reminded himself now, changing position so his leg wouldn't fall asleep on the damp ground. Or if you do, make it the kind of joke that begins, "a priest, a rabbi, and a minister walk into a bar…" Something on the idiot's level.

Because joke with an idiot about "tails," and you might find yourself receiving a surprise package from Federal Express containing the rear business of three Orange-spotted Western newts. And the local talk shows might start ranting about the sick individual going around mutilating tiny helpless endangered reptiles, and the politicians might start demanding a full investigation.

So here he was. With a trap. And bait.

He sat and he waited. And he felt it again. That sense that he was being watched. That there were other eyes here, and not the eyes of gentle marsh creatures either. Human eyes. Which didn't wish Clyde Arbuckle well.

Guido Pirelli, the well-known orthopedic surgeon, flung the 3x7 inch black plastic box, the one which had destroyed his life, against the wall. But unlike Guido's poor heart, it didn't shatter—only cracked a little in one corner, and bounced onto the floor.

How he wished he could rewind this day, the way he'd rewound that tape; rewind it to the moment before "a friend" had slipped that envelope through Pirelli's mail slot; the moment before Guido Pirelli had learned of Love's Dark Side.

For he had truly loved Susanna, loved her at first sight, if you come down to it, although he hadn't realized it at the time. At the time, he'd attributed the sweating, the rapid pulse, the dizziness he felt in her presence to indigestion, or to early signs of the heart disease which ran in his family. He'd been 60 years old, after all. He'd had no reason to suspect that, at that relatively advanced age and for the first time in his life, he'd just been felled by the thunderbolt.

When Guido was a young boy, and beginning to show an interest in girls, his father Luigi had taken him aside and warned him of this thunderbolt; the deadly passion that will happen to a man, and which he can no more resist that he can resist the tides or an erupting volcano. Guido must take care, Luigi had said, since Italians were more susceptible to it than the colder-blooded races. (The Swedes and the Norwegians were practically immune, according to Luigi, which might explain why the Italians invented Grand Opera, while the Swedes invented pickled herring.)

But no thunderbolt had ever stricken Guido Pirelli.

Certainly not when he'd met his first wife Maria. She had been attractive in the dark way he liked, and good-natured, and a wonderful cook. He'd married her for her osso bucco, and never regretted it. They'd had 32 good years together, years filled with scallopine and marinara; with clams casino and chicken parmesan, and this isn't even counting her desserts. A man could have loved her for her cannoli alone.

And Guido had loved her, in his way, but it was an easy, quiet sort of love, which never disturbed his equanimity.

After she died, and a proper period of mourning had passed, Guido had had other women. Actually, he'd had other women even while Maria was alive, though these had been mainly what you might call targets of opportunity—an adoring nurse, an eager pharmaceutical rep. He didn't chase women; he acquiesced to them. He was courtly, generous, fluent in the language of romantic gestures. But he'd felt little for his mistresses beyond an agreeable tickle of desire, and a certain muted pleasure in their company.

And then one fateful day, Susanna O'Shaughnessy tripped on a fake Oriental rug in a model home, and broke her leg in two places—this was during her brief, unsuccessful career in real estate—, and Guido had been called in to consult. It wasn't her beauty that had attracted him. She wasn't beautiful.

Even his love-blinded, age-dimmed eyes could tell that. And if he had any doubt— "her head is too big for her body," his daughter Louise had pointed out. "She looks like a lollipop."

But to Guido, Susanna had something better than beauty, more interesting than charm. She had that fatal combination of alluring coldness and ravening sexual appetite, common, Guido suspected, to many of the great enchantresses of history, (such as Cleopatra).

Not that it mattered what Susanna had or didn't have. The thunderbolt struck Guido Pirelli, and so he married Susanna, against the advice of his friends, and over the violent objections of his children, who considered her, correctly, nothing more than a common little gold-digger.

And although she wouldn't play pinochle or accompany him to *The Barber of Seville*; although she sometimes referred to him as Pops and her idea of cuisine was a peanut butter and jelly sandwich, he adored her, and for the first three years of their marriage Guido Pirelli was a very happy man.

For Susanna was a maestro of sex. Love with her was love, but it was also music, and with an ever-changing repertoire. Sometimes Chopin, delicate and meditative; sometimes Wagner, soaring from crescendo to crescendo; sometimes the down-and-dirty rhythms of rock and roll.

He had heard rumors, of course, almost since Susanna had won elective office, (thanks to his financial support); rumors about her and this man or that man, most recently that new Chief of County Operations, Bill somebody or other. She had warned Guido to expect this. People are always ready to slander a strong and powerful woman, she'd said.

Guido supposed this was true, though he could never

remember hearing rumors like that about Margaret Thatcher, for instance, or Golda Meir. Nevertheless he kept any doubts he might have had to himself. What is marriage without trust, he told himself, the same thing he used to tell Maria when she wondered why he sometimes came home smelling of cheap perfume, and with lipstick on his shirt.

But even lovesick Guido couldn't deny the evidence of his own eyes—could it be just five minutes ago—up there on the screen: Susanna nuzzling Bill Washington, her arm around his waist as the automatic doors of the Comfort Inn slid open to receive them.

An old fool. That's what Louise had called him. An old fool. It was at moments like this that he wished he really had been Sicilian; that his father and grandfather really had broken bones for a living, while he mended them, instead of it just being a joke he made (a stupid joke, Susanna said). In fact, his forebears had owned a cheese shop in Florence, and had never done anything more antisocial than overcharging for a mediocre mascarpone.

A Sicilian would have known exactly what to do in this situation, the good doctor thought; probably something involving dismembered bodies in a ravine, or torsos dissolved in a vat of sulfuric acid.

But this was not Guido's refined, Northern Italian way. He required something more subtle than dismemberment, but equally sufficient to slake his thirst for revenge.

Maybe it was another sign of age, but Carole couldn't think

of anything she'd rather be doing right now than sitting on a folding camp stool in this marsh, studying Dennis' rounded back as he scrutinized the reeds through his binoculars.

What was it about a man's bent back that could make him seem so touchingly vulnerable, she wondered, that could bring to mind the appealing boy he must once have been? She remembered that day at the lake with her son Patrick, when Patrick was seven. A quiet solitary child, he'd hunched by the water's edge throwing stones, while she watched him from a blanket. In his delicate, exposed spine she seemed to see all the sorrow his body would bring him later on, all the inevitable heartbreak. And she'd had a preposterous impulse to stop it, this terrible unfolding of genetic necessity; to gather him back into her womb where she could keep him safe from harm and disappointment forever.

He grew up anyway, into a green-haired, lip-ringed, never-held-a-job-for-more-than-three-months stranger she didn't particularly like. Carole reassured herself that of course she still loved him, though if pressed to define it, Carole would have had a hard time saying exactly what this love consisted of, beyond a bittersweet memory of a boy's back on the beach, and a willingness to bail her son out of jail should the need arise.

She coughed.

"How much longer do you think we should wait for him to show up?"

Not that she believed for a minute that Clyde Arbuckle himself would come skulking around the marsh, looking to slice-and-dice another Orange-spotted Western newt. Even if he were behind the mysterious mutilations, he would have cleverly insulated himself from the dirty deed, the same way he cleverly insulated himself from all his other dirty deeds. The newt-psycho-killer would turn out to be some offshore corporation, owned by another offshore corporation...

Carole had come along not to catch Arbuckle, but for the adventure, and because Dennis had invited her. "I have a date with Dennis," she'd told Henry, not that he asked. Henry was used to her doing things without him. In fact, they rarely did things together anymore, so she didn't know why she'd made such a point of saying she had a date with Dennis, and made such a joke of it besides. Have fun, Henry had said, not even looking up from one of the three newspapers he read every day, now that he was retired.

He didn't just skim them either. He digested them like a python methodically devouring a pig. Riots in Indonesia. Electoral fraud in Mozambique. Drought in Zimbabwe. Unimportant countries everybody else skipped on their way to the funnies. Now Henry had become an expert on their individual variations on the general theme of national catastrophe.

There are grave water shortages in sub-Saharan Africa, he'd announce. The village wells are dry. The cattle are dying. He didn't sound especially alarmed by this, but more as though he were passing along an interesting tidbit of information, like Mickey Mantle's lifetime batting average.

Which is why it had taken her by surprise this afternoon, when Henry said he was thinking of joining the Senior Peace Corps. You would think that after 30 years of marriage, you could count on a man not to suddenly go all peculiar on you.

But peculiar is what Henry definitely was becoming. Just a week ago she'd found him in his workshop, sawing a 2 by

4, stark naked. When she'd asked him why, he would only say that it felt good, that it was something he'd never tried before, and he wanted to do it once before he died, to live on the edge.

She wondered what else was on his list of things to do before he died, and hoped most of them could be accomplished fully clothed. Henry's pear-shaped, nearly hairless body hadn't been a thing of beauty even in the flower of his youth. At 58, it resembled a pale pink hot water bottle, stretched flaccid by overuse.

I have a date with Dennis, she'd said.

Enjoy yourself, he'd said.

Henry probably didn't realize that "dating" now meant "having sex." When they were young, dating had been what you did while you *considered* having sex. Was she considering having sex with Dennis? Is that why she'd called it a date? She didn't think so—at least not sex as is in heaving and humping and exchanges of body fluids and the routine disappointment of male nakedness.

But she had a definite longing to run her hand over his back, and a vision of her and Dennis on a couch, watching "Masterpiece Theater" together, her feet in his lap, him gently rubbing her arches. And then he lifts the foot and presses his mouth to her ankle, and runs his tongue up her bare calf...

And now here they were, alone together on a summer evening, the air like a warm fragrant blanket, the birds beginning their twilight songs. What if she were to casually graze his back with her fingertips, she wondered? She could always pretend it was an accident. But that wasn't what she wanted. She wanted to linger there, to memorize each subtle undulation of his vertebrae. And there was no way to disguise that as an accident, or as anything but what it was—desire. Desire. At her age. She felt ridiculous, but also she felt something else...

Alive—that was it. She felt alive. And how much longer did she have even to be alive, much less feel alive? So if she didn't reach out now, in the magic of a perfumed summer night, she could be dead before she got another chance. She would go home to Henry and his melancholy silences and the vast empty spaces yawning between them like the dark matter of an ever-expanding universe....

She stretched her arm...there, there...almost there...

"Shh...," Dennis murmurred. "Did you hear that?"

He turned around. His lips brushed her fingers.

"Oops, sorry," he giggled.

Oh that giggle. Carole winced. When Dennis was uneasy around people, which was most of the time, a high-pitched giggle would punctuate his speech like a self-deprecating dash or a superfluous comma. She'd mentioned it to him once, tactfully she hoped, how those little mid-sentence barks of his made him seem overly apologetic, and caused people to take him less seriously than he deserved.

The mannerism had almost disappeared after that, at least when they were alone together. She hoped the mere touch of her fingers hadn't made him backslide. Or rather, she hoped it had.

"Lose the giggle Dennis," she whispered.

"Huh?"

"The giggle, lose it."

And then she kissed him PLONK on the mouth.

It had been over thirty years since she'd last had a first kiss, and she couldn't remember exactly what was supposed to happen next. In the movies—nowadays—the first kiss would be followed by the immediate tearing off of clothing, and then a lot of thrashing around, and then the pulled-up sheets, and the afterglow. She didn't think that was on the agenda here—certainly not on her agenda.

"Carole," Dennis moaned, "Carole, Carole Carole." He held her wrists and pressed his forehead to hers.

"Do you have any idea how long I have worshiped you?"

They moved toward each other and kissed again. She could taste his peppermint-flavored teeth.

And that's when they heard the terrible scream.

You're lucky to still be alive," the doctor had told Clyde Arbuckle when Clyde first had emerged into consciousness, not knowing where he was or remembering how he'd gotten there. The last thing Clyde remembered was the sudden, excruciating pain and an awful sound, which he now realized must have been coming from deep inside himself, from some place of unimaginable agony.

Then the doctor had showed him where to push the button on the pump "when the pain got too bad." Since Clyde was a great big coward when it came to pain—he had been known to cry like a baby over an ice cream headache—Clyde found himself pushing the button a lot. And was pleasantly surprised to find that when he did this, not only did he not feel the pain, but he felt the happiest he'd ever felt in his life.

Which is how Clyde Arbuckle came, by accident, and at

the ripe age of 45, to his very first experience of chemical bliss.

For early on, when his high school classmates were busily zoning out on marijuana, or drinking themselves into stupors, Clyde had decided that if he were to make his way in this cruel world, he could afford only one serious vice, and that vice had better be avarice. Later, in college, when he began to waver, when he found himself gazing wistfully out his dormitory window at the carefree fraternity boys staggering home from some wild party, laughing and barfing, he would remember his father Calvin Arbuckle's parting advice: "You snooze," Calvin had said, "you lose." And Calvin should know. It had been Calvin's own alcohol-fueled snoozing which had caused him to overlook his partner's systematic embezzlement, and had led to the ruin of the Arbuckle family fortunes.

And so it happened that Clyde Arbuckle had wasted the best years of his life stone cold sober.

Now he smiled, a goofy smile which had not been seen on Clyde's pudgy face since infancy.

He leaned over, anxious to start the sweet drip coursing again through his eager veins. Already he could feel a throbbing sensation somewhere in the neighborhood of his ankle.

But someone was grabbing Clyde's arm before Clyde could reach the button.

"It might be a good idea to let up on that a little."

A doctor stood by his bedside, a different doctor, a smooth-cheeked twerp who looked barely old enough to be dispensing McBurgers, much less McMedical advice. Maybe this wasn't a real doctor at all, Clyde thought hopefully. Maybe it was some kid impersonating a doctor as a college prank.

Clyde snorted.

"No sonny boy, I don't think it would be a good idea to let up on that a little, and if you don't get your fucking hands off of me this minute, I'm going to have to report you to the principal," Clyde tittered. "Do you realize who I am?"

Dr. Twerp picked up the chart attached to the foot of the bed, and coldly recited:

"Arbuckle, Clyde D, 45-year-old, obese Caucasian male, admitted with acute poisoning as a result of unknown toxin. Brought in by Dennis Mulnick, no relation, who reported discovering patient delirious and in extreme distress at Rubin's Marsh. Mulnick applied first aid at the scene after concluding that patient had suffered possible snakebite; cut open puncture, sucked out venom through tube and applied tourniquet. Patient in shock on admission to emergency room and had defecated and urinated in clothing…"

Clyde waved his hand imperiously, still with something of his usual air of command—granted it isn't easy to feel all that commanding in front of a person who is telling you how you crapped your pants, and they had to put you in the super-jumbo-size Depends.

The doctor closed the chart.

"Would you like to meet the man who saved your life, Mr. Arbuckle?"

Clyde didn't think so. He'd never had much use for do-gooders.

But it was too late. Even as the doctor spoke, the venom-sucking hero was striding through the door. He looked familiar—this Mulnick—or maybe it was just that Clyde recognized the type: lean and sinewy, plaid shirt, neatly pressed denims, fisherman's hat, little pepper-and-salt beard, bike clip on the trousers. There were always a bunch of them showing up at Council meetings to protest Arbuckle's projects, and to sing, "We shall Overcome" and "This land is my land." Like it was still the fucking Sixties.

Clyde slunk deep under the thin waffle-weave hospital blanket. He didn't like the idea of this Mr. Eagle Scout Kumbaya Mulnick slobbering all over him and telling him what a GREAT privilege it had been to save Clyde's life, though Clyde suspected that this type valued the life of an owl, or even a salamander, more than it valued the life of a Clyde Arbuckle.

The throbbing in Clyde's leg was getting worse, quickly approaching unbearable. He reached for the pump again, but the doctor had already disconnected it from the IV line, and moved it away, out of Clyde's reach. Clyde began to pant hard. Sweat poured down his face.

When the young doctor left, Clyde quickly swiveled himself over the side of the bed. He'd go get the pump himself, fuck it. But as he attempted to heave the great bulk of his upper body onto his legs, he began to crumble as if he were a pyramid built on stilts, and a ferocious burning tore at his calf. Gasping, he rolled back into prone position. All right then. Plan B. Though he had taken an instant dislike to this Mulnick, he would have to appeal to Mulnick's common decency. This type, in Clyde's experience, tended to have common decency up the yingyang, and weren't afraid to let you know it either.

"Would you mind very much moving that closer?" Clyde whimpered, with as much heartrending pathos as he could manage, given that he felt as if his head were about to implode. "I'm really *really* suffering here."

"Move what?" Mulnick had a peculiar stretched smile on his face, a smile that said to Clyde not, "it was a privilege saving your life," but something more along the lines of, "I would like to see you die horribly, choking on your own vomit." Arbuckle ought to know. He'd seen that look, or something similar, many times before. You didn't get to be Clyde Arbuckle without making a few enemies.

Mulnick shook his head.

"Oh I see, you mean the morphine, you'd like me to move over the *morphine*?

"Morphine? Is that what it is?" Clyde's arms reached out towards the blessed stuff, as if he could attract it through sheer willpower.

"Sorry," Mulnick shrugged," I just don't see how I can do that."

"You don't think you can do that?" Clyde screamed. Where Clyde's nervous system formerly had been were one million horrible gnawing little worms. "Have you ever been bitten by a snake, you fucking holier-than-shit save-the-striped-baboon-son-of-a-bitch. Do you have any idea how excruciating it is?"

Mulnick sat in the green vinyl chair next to the bed, and calmly folded his arms across his chest. He removed a piece of paper from his fanny pack.

"No I haven't been bitten by a snake," he said, "and Mr. Arbuckle, neither have you."

"What are you talking about?" Clyde sputtered. "It says right in the chart that it was a snake."

Mulnick brought his face near to Clyde's. Clyde had never gotten this close to one of these people before, but it came as no surprise to him, that Mulnick's breath smelled of something faintly herbal.

"It was the Orange-spotted newt that got you, Arbuckle, nearly making you extinct, while you were trying to nearly make *it* extinct." Mulnick waved his finger at Clyde's nose. "Not only a despicable, a morally indefensible act, but also, as it happens, a crime punishable by a substantial fine and a term in a Federal penitentiary."

Clyde shivered in the overheated room. Prison. Mulnick couldn't seriously be talking about prison. For what? For attempted murder of a lizard? Still, if there was even the slightest chance—his throat constricted as he recalled everything he'd heard about what went on in the "joint." If there's one thing Clyde was a bigger coward about than pain, it was getting sodomized by large men with tattoos.

"What do you want from me Mulnick?" he groaned. "Anything. Anything."

The other nodded and inched the pump a little closer.

He handed Arbuckle a pen and a piece of paper.

He hooked up the pump.

Sign here, he said.

And Clyde Arbuckle did.

And signed again. And again.

When the two police officers banged on Bill Washington's door and handed him the warrant, he figured it at first for some kind of practical joke. He wouldn't have put it past Hansen, or even that wacko Bradbury over in Finance to concoct a scheme like this to make him look ridiculous. He knew he wasn't popular with the civil service rank-and-file—the price you pay for being a strong leader. So any minute now he expected the "officers" to start bumping and grinding, tearing off their fake uniforms, and shouting, "let's par-tay." The jokester—Hansen or Bradbury or whoever—was probably hiding in the bushes right now, waiting for Washington to soil his shorts. Well Washington would show whoever it was that two could play at this game.

"Ooh, officers," he cooed, rubbing the bicep of the closer one, whose 'badge' identified him as 'Buster'—clearly not his real name—"what big muscles you have."

This didn't sit well with 'Buster', who grabbed Washington's arms and handcuffed them behind Washington's back, which was carrying the joke a little too far, in Washington's opinion. "Fun's fun, guys," he said, "but any more rough stuff, and I'm going to have to call the real cops."

Upon which Buster dragged Washington over to a Crown Vic which looked remarkably like a genuine patrol vehicle, while Buster's partner smashed the lock on Washington's storage shed and emerged waving two bedraggled plants Washington had never seen before.

"Plenty more where these came from," the partner shouted. "Whole fucking industrial-strength operation in there."

And that's when Washington realized he was in deep shit. She'd framed him, the bitch, just because he'd finally gotten the *cojones* to break it off. Well if he was going down, he was dragging her down with him. He knew where the bodies were buried, oh yes, right there stinking to high heaven on his hard drive: Susanna Pirelli's e-mails, concerning what she wanted him to do for Clyde Arbuckle, and what Arbuckle would do in return, and the meetings at the Red Horse. And that's not even counting the just plain filthy and disgusting stuff.

"Officer Buster," he said. "I think you just might wanna take along my laptop while you're at it."

When the call came from the mayor's office, Councilwoman Susanna Pirelli had been sitting at her desk thinking about her husband Guido, and especially about Guido's strange behavior the night before, actually his strange behavior for over a week now.

Little things mostly. Like him not kissing his fingertips to her as he left for work. Or not pouring her coffee for her at breakfast, carefully measuring the cream with one of the silver spoons he'd inherited from his grandmother. Or that he suddenly had started wearing flannel pajamas to bed, claiming to feel chilly though it was only September. She worried her hold on him might be slipping. She knew the signs. So last night she had even offered *Ravel's Bolero* sex, Guido's favorite sex, though Susanna herself considered it a little corny and obvious—those trite overlapping crescendos, those shmaltzy violins—, and as a rule only offered *Bolero* sex when she wanted something from Guido really badly.

Last night Guido had turned her down flat. Claimed he was too tired.

She took a hand mirror out of her pocketbook, and studied the face she'd recently remodeled at great cost and expense. She wondered if it'd been worth the Act 2 of *Tosca* she'd put out for it. Yes, the sags and the wrinkles were all gone, but maybe it was true, what she'd overheard the young receptionist telling the new administrative assistant: that Councilwoman Pirelli looked like her face had gotten caught in a Category Three hurricane.

She seemed to be losing her touch with men.

Bill Washington had gone and dumped her, inventing some story about how he was considering taking a position in Kuala Lumpur. And even before Arbuckle got bit by the snake, she practically had to use a vacuum cleaner hose to give him a hard on...

So she had a lot on her mind when the mayor called, and it took her a while to take in what he was saying. Something about e-mails retrieved from a hard drive, and bribery, and Arbuckle City. And only when he got to the part about secret meetings at the Red Horse did Susanna realize the mayor was talking about her, and that her entire world had just come to an end.

"COUNTY BIGWIGS CHARGED IN DRUG/CORRUPTION SCANDAL"

Guido Pirelli closed the newspaper. A job well done, he thought, and worth the price.

The man had called Guido not long after the tape had been shoved through Guido's mail slot. Would Guido like to get his revenge on Susanna's lover, the man had asked? And before Guido could say, "sorry, I'm not that kind of cuckold," the man—who had a faint foreign accent Guido couldn't quite place—was explaining how he would trick-wire Washington's house; how the Seek and Destroy computers would pick up the surge; then the man would sneak the marijuana plants into Washington's shed, and would phone in an anonymous tip just to make sure...all for a bargain basement $10,000. What's $10,000 to Guido, the man asked—a compound fracture? Half of a hip replacement?

It was the irony of it that had appealed to Guido, for Guido not only had the soul of a poet (like most Italians), but also, in certain respects, the sensibility of a late Twentieth Century post-modern novelist.

Seek and Destroy had been the proudest achievement of Susanna's political career. She boasted about it all the time, how she was going to stamp out the evil of pot-farming in our County in our lifetime.

So it pleased him, the irony of it, that Seek and Destroy ultimately sought and destroyed not only Bill Washington, but Susanna herself.

It was so…Florentine!

Carole should have been more surprised to find the note, but in a way she had been expecting it for a long time. Henry had always been a man of few words, and wasn't it just like him to end a 30-year marriage with:

"Moved to Alabama to work with Habitat for Humanity. Best wishes, Henry. P.S. you can have everything."

She knew she probably should call the children, but why bother them right now? They had their own busy complicated lives. Patrick's band, *Scrambled Brains*, was on tour. Lizzie and her girlfriend, Celeste, were busy remodeling the old farmhouse in upstate New York where they planned to hold the wedding ceremony next summer. Jody, their youngest, was in Spain on his junior year abroad, and recently had started experimenting with, of all things, Catholicism. It's a phase, Henry had assured her. It will pass. And then Henry revealed that he had been attracted to the Catholic faith at one time himself, and had even considered entering the priesthood. This surprised her. Just as there are people you can't imagine having sex—people who are really really good at math, for instance—there are people you can't imagine hankering after God, and Henry was one of those. How little we really know each other, she thought, a thought no less true for being so painfully obvious.

There would be plenty of time to call the children. For all she knew Henry might've called them already.

She would call Dennis instead.

They'd barely spoken since that night at the marsh three weeks ago. You practically had to make an appointment to speak to Dennis Melnick now. He had to squeeze you in, between the interviews with the newsmagazines and the appearances on "Good Morning America" and so forth. "In a nation which is hungry for heroes," the perky hostess would bubble, "we're proud to have a real one here with us today; a man who, at great risk to his own life, saved the life of a man whose mega-developments he'd been protesting for over a decade." Then the tycoon signs over the deed to Robinson's Marsh out of sheer gratitude. Plus agrees to convert a half-dozen luxury condo complexes into low-income housing. That's what gave the story its legs, that "love thine enemy" angle. That sound-bite redemption.

Carole alone knew that Dennis actually had hesitated for a beat when he saw who it was lying there, writhing in pain, and had even started to walk away. Then Dennis' bedrock decency had kicked in, and he began ripping his own undershirt to make a tourniquet. Dennis had been magnificent, utterly composed, utterly sure of himself, as if he had been in training for this moment since his first day in Boy Scouts; had been carrying around that old snakebite kit for a quarter-century, just in case.

Women were throwing themselves at him.

On the call-in shows, honeysuckle-voiced ladies would wonder if he was married. They'd offer to send him a picture, a phone number, panties.

It seemed so unfair. Carole had appreciated Dennis when nobody else had. It was Carole who had seen his potential, under the comb-over, the dingy teeth, the white socks, the irritating tics. It had been Carole who, with her gentle prodding and tactful reminders of his faults, had turned him into a more or less viable specimen of a man. And now that he was all that, and a hero besides, was she about to lose him to little Miss Moonlight-and-Magnolias from Tuscaloosa? Not if she could help it.

She picked up the phone, and pressed his number on the autodial.

He was at her house a half-hour later.

He handed her flowers and a bottle of wine. His russet eyes glowed.

He took her in his arms.

Do you have any idea, he said, how long I have worshiped you?

"If you'd been keeping your eye on the ball, Wolf," Ted Hutchinson drawled, his voice thick with his usual sarcasm, "maybe you wouldn't have missed the boat in the first place."

The City Editor was mixing his metaphors again, Jason noticed, one of the reasons Jason had trouble respecting the man. And where did he dig up that jacket—from a Salvation Army bin? Who says a good reporter has to look like he slept in his clothes? Jason himself was always careful to avoid the rumpled, stained-tie stereotype, if only to show respect for his sources. Not that Jason had any sources at present, but if he ever did…

Just like Hutchinson to rub it in, Jason thought, as if Jason didn't feel bad enough already. It would figure that the one Planning Commission meeting Jason decided to skip was the meeting where they had approved the preliminary permit for Arbuckle City, to be constructed on the site of Robinson's Marsh. If Jason had been there, Jason was confident his journalistic instincts would have smelled a rat: a story, as it turned out, with everything—bribery, corruption, sex, money, snakes. And what had Jason done instead? Gone on a blind date with that Allison chick who told him five minutes in that she thought he'd make a great friend, but that she was just getting over a painful breakup, and wasn't ready to get involved. Blahblahblah. Jason knew the drill. Knew it by heart.

Oh well. At least he was making progress on that other

investigation.

Jason opened the folder where he kept the clippings, neatly arranged in chronological order.

From the *St Paul Leader*:

Dateline: Duluth:

Bazooms, the restaurant chain famous for its scantily clad waitresses and bottomless buckets of chicken wings, announced it is closing its one remaining franchise in Duluth due to what management termed "a shifting customer base." One laid-off staffer, speaking on condition of anonymity, blamed Bazooms' problems on its sudden, unexplained popularity with a new demographic.

"They come ten at a time, and the first thing they do is they want you to, like, turn down the music. Then they order the house salad, dressing on the side, and pay with, like, ten separate credit cards, leave s**t for tips, and all of a sudden—hey—like all the dudes disappear, like they suddenly saw their, like, GRANDMOTHER..."

This follows the shuttering of Bazooms locations in Tampa, Louisville and Phoenix under similar circumstances. The stock of Bazooms' parent company, Scarfandleer Inc., fell 20 points on the news...

From the *Daily Mail*

Dateline: London:

"Our names are Gert and Priscilla: we rob banks."

That's what the note read, written in what Scotland Yard's Chief Superintendent Jane Featherstone describes as "really beautiful old-fashioned penmanship."

But no one knows the true identities of the pair of Queen Mum look-alikes who hit a Hampstead Heath Barclays branch yesterday afternoon. Wearing flowered dresses, sensible shoes and white gloves, and waving small pearl-handled revolvers, they collected their loot in what one baffled teller described as "very nice" patent leather handbags with gold clasps.

Complicating the CID's task is the fact that the dozens of customers who caught a glimpse of the robbers can agree only that the women were "nondescript."

Said manager Giles Throckmorton, "They were extremely polite, real ladies. It was a pleasure doing business with them."

And a dozen more like it. Women of a certain age, all over the world, acting completely out of character. Coincidence? Jason didn't think so.

His reporter's sixth sense told him that somehow these were all connected. And connected also to that lawyer and the infomercial. He couldn't have said why he felt they were connected. He just had this hunch that he was on to something BIG. And that this something could be the making of Jason Wolf, Investigative Journalist.

"BIGWIGS CHARGED IN DRUG/CORRUPTION SCANDAL"

Arabella Wolf put down her *Afternoon Gazette*. It depressed her, as usual. All that delicious wickedness in the world just crying out to be exposed, and there was Jason stuck covering the boring old Zoning Board, or whatever they called it.

He had to start somewhere, he'd told her. She supposed so, but she hoped he'd go somewhere else soon, somewhere that paid better.

Arabella had supported her son's journalistic ambitions ever since he'd edited his fifth grade newsletter, *Class Notes,* and unmasked that lunch-swapping ring. She only wished she weren't actually *supporting* his ambitions. She hadn't counted on Jason's moving back in after graduate school, upsetting her plans to convert his old bedroom to a home gym.

That was before she'd broken her leg falling off the treadmill at Pure Fitness, of course. Now about the only exercise she got was clicking the mouse on her new computer.

She sighed. Two months since the accident, and Arabella already had lost much of her hard-earned muscle tone. She noted, with special disgust, the quivering jelly where her biceps used to be. Enough! Even if she couldn't use the treadmill, she could at least do something about her upper body. She hobbled over to the computer, and typed the words "flabby arms" in the little box where it said 'Google.'

Melissa Crane turned on the machine.

"So that's how Jason Wolf put it all together, his mother just happening to stumble across your website?"

"Calltoflabbyarms.com? Well that too, but mainly this other thing... having to do with Janet."

"Janet? But I thought Janet was..."

"Our moral compass? Oh yes, but she eventually became so much more than that. You'll be surprised to learn, for instance, that it was Janet who committed our first actual felony. Only a class C felony maybe, but still, who would have expected even that from Janet Miller? She wasn't exactly the type, if you know what I mean. She was the type who served meals at the homeless shelter on Thanksgiving. The type who would spend summer vacations in some impoverished country teaching the villagers how to dig latrines. But that was before...

"But I should go back and begin at the beginning, I suppose, with Danny Higgins, the thieving contractor. Janet had inherited this money from her Aunt Millie, see, and decided to use it to remodel the master bath, which was not at all like Janet, and really put her husband Eric's nose out of joint..."

Book Three
Janet

Chapter Six

Janet Stays Home

Janet didn't know why she'd bothered staying home to wait for Danny, again. For three months now he'd been promising to come by and fix the tile work in the master bath, where he'd managed to install a decorative ceramic frieze upside down. He refused to admit it was his fault, of course. Nothing was ever Danny's fault. This time blame fell on the manufacturer, who'd failed to mark the preferred orientation of the tiles.

But even Eric, a man who had been known to go to work wearing one black shoe and one brown shoe, could sense something wasn't right.

"Doesn't the flower part usually go *over* the stem part?"

Not anymore, Danny had said. Now anything could go anywhere—implying the problem was not so much his ineptitude, as their lack of imagination. Still, if they weren't happy, he'd come back and redo it, he offered. It was important to him that they be satisfied. Janet was beginning to suspect that wasn't the case; that what was important to Danny was to take the money and vanish. Sandi had warned her that this was often the way of things with contractors. This was why you always held back half the price until the job was completed. Sandi was right. Sandi was usually right about practical matters. Janet had too soft a heart for her own good, in Sandi's opinion, and people took advantage.

"Thank God you didn't pay the final installment," Sandi had said, surveying the upended tulips on the bathroom wall, the crooked cabinet, the off-center sink.

"Hmm," Janet had replied, hoping Sandi wouldn't cross-examine her the way she sometimes did. Because when Danny had asked Janet for an advance to pay for his son's costly drug rehabilitation program, she just hadn't had the heart to say no. Besides, Danny told her, she knew she could trust him to come back and finish up the final details.

Three months and four missed appointments later, Janet was beginning to suspect that wasn't the case; that what she could trust Danny to do was to cash the check and never be seen again.

Rule Number One: Do not make friends with your contractor.

They'd warned her—Sandi and Ellie both—like veteran mothers preparing the first timer for the agonies of childbirth: Remodeling is Hell.

But Janet had hoped it would be easier for her, because she wasn't a control freak, like Sandi, or a perfectionist, like Ellie. When Ellie told Janet her home improvement horror stories —that's what Ellie called them, "horror stories"—Janet found that her sympathies were often with the workmen, with Ellie's long-suffering painter, for instance, who had had to redo a hallway three times before he was able to achieve the correct shade of pale khaki. Khaki was hard, Ellie explained. Khaki, some people felt, was pretty near impossible. But done right, Ellie insisted, it could be truly elegant.

Janet never would even have *attempted* khaki. After one early misadventure with a bedroom color called "lemon meringue," which had made her feel as if she were sleeping inside a hard-boiled egg, Janet had stuck to reliable off-whites, to "ivory" or "Belgian lace." She lacked basic confidence in her design instincts, or in her instincts for anything else having to do with the general field of gracious living. This she blamed mainly on her upbringing.

For while Ellie (who did not only khaki, but everything else right) had been raised by a former debutante, Janet's mother Ida had been a Communist, whose idea of home improvement was to tack a picture of Lenin over the cracks in the plaster. Janet grew up eating mismatched food—spaghetti with sweet potatoes, for instance—off mismatched plates, and the clothes Ida bought her at the Socialist Workers' Thrift Shop were always a size too big or a size too small, and were never entirely pressed or truly clean.

Janet loved her parents. She admired them. Even today, 85 years old and living in a mature adult community in Boca Raton, they still were fighting to make the world a better place—Saul leading the campaign for properly functioning elevators in Building B; Ida, a late-life convert to proper nutrition, insisting on vegetarian options in the Meals on Wheels program.

But it was no wonder, Janet thought, given the way she'd been reared, that she could be intimidated to the point of despair by a rack of paint samples. No wonder her T-shirts always wrinkled, even when she used the permanent press cycle and removed them from the dryer the instant the buzzer sounded. No wonder when, for the first time in her life, she attempted to remodel a bathroom, nothing turned out exactly right. Or even inexactly right. We weren't talking impossible things, she fumed, such as khaki, we were talking *tulips*, which could be done right by the average six-year-old.

But not, apparently, by Disappearing Danny.

Eric told her to forget about it. What was the big deal? He'd been against the project from the beginning. There were more important things they could do with the $20,000 inheritance from her aunt Millie, he'd said, than to beautify a room in which they spent maybe half an hour a day. Was it more important that Janet have heated towel bars than that the Sierra Club continue its battle against strip mining in West Virginia? That Janet soak in a sage-green Jacuzzi tub, than that a child be rescued from a carpet factory in Pakistan where little girls were chained to their looms and went blind by age eleven?

Millie would have voted for the tub, Janet had replied. By opting for it herself, she argued, she was honoring her aunt's memory.

When Janet was a little girl, Ida would take her once a year to visit Millie's tiny Upper West Side apartment, a den of frivolity where every flat surface was encrusted with half-empty perfume bottles, gauzy glittery scarves, shiny pink satin undergarments trimmed in cheap lace, clumps of rhinestone earrings, fake eyelashes, fabric-covered high-heeled shoes, crocks filled with dusty, sweet-smelling face powder. Aunt Millie's studio had been a place of mysterious feminine glamour and allure to little Janet, a fit setting for Aunt Millie herself, who, to Janet's nearsighted eyes, resembled a short, Jewish, Rita Hayworth.

"*Dreck*," Ida would spit afterwards. "*Chazerei.* My sister hasn't got a pot to piss in, and still she spends money on that *dreck* and *chazerei*."

While as a rule, the fact that a person lacked a pot to piss in only increased Ida's esteem for that person, she made an exception in Millie's case. Ida even hinted that some of the *dreck* in question (in particular the pink satin, lace-trimmed *dreck*) had actually been a gift from Mr. Birnbaum, Millie's boss at Birnbaum International, the import-export firm where Millie worked as an executive secretary. Ida never actually used the word "affair" (being a puritanical-type Communist, not a free-love-type Communist), but Janet had known what Ida meant: Millie was in love with Mr. Birnbaum, who was married and lived in Westchester. And in fact, after Birnbaum's wife passed on, he and Millie began living openly in sin, or in as much sin as they could manage at 78 and 76 respectively. Which Janet considered a happy ending, and Ida considered vindication. When Birnbaum died a few bliss-filled years later, he left Millie quite well off, which is how Millie happened to have $20,000 to leave Janet in the first place.

Janet and Eric had argued about the bathroom for months. Ordinarily Janet would have capitulated. She'd known when she'd married him all those years ago that Eric was a compulsive philanthropist. That's what she'd loved about him, wasn't it—his unrelenting goodness?

Only she was beginning to get a little tired of it by now. Sometimes she wished, just once, that he would buy her pink satin underwear trimmed in lace, or even a bottle of perfume. His gifts were always so practical. On Valentine's Day last year he'd given her a clip-on book light so she could read in bed without disturbing his sleep. Thoughtful, yes, but still...

So this one time she held her ground, and finally, they'd compromised. Janet would get her updated bath. Eric would get to award the job to someone who really needed it, rather than to someone who, for example, actually knew what he was doing.

Rule Number Two: Never hire a contractor for reasons of conscience.

Eric had found Danny Higgins through a program called "Fresh Start," which helped ex-cons reintegrate into the community. Danny was one of their great success stories. After serving a prison term Danny described as 'brief,' for an offense Danny described as 'nonviolent,' he'd built up a flourishing home repair and improvement business, which now employed three of his former cell-mates. And to top it off, Danny claimed to be one-eighth Navajo on his mother's side.

"You'll love this guy," Eric had told her. "He's the real thing."

Certainly no one could accuse Danny of being slick or over-packaged. From the long grey-streaked ponytail to the beer belly drooped over the tooled leather belt to the tobacco-stained fingers and the grimy Sears work boots, Danny oozed been-to-the-bottom-and-bounced-back-up-again authenticity.

And he *sounded* like he knew what he was doing: throwing around words like 'fascia' and 'cost-plus,' criticizing the workmanship of prior contractors, observing that the wiring was not up to code, and that the plumbing was the old-fashioned zinc-copper alloy nobody used anymore.

And he *looked* like he knew what he was doing: measuring things with the steel tape measure hooked to his belt, jotting notes in a notebook, creeping under sinks, crawling into crawl spaces.

It was only when Danny actually *did* something that it became clear he had no idea what he was doing. When every pipe leaked and had to be re-soldered. When the cabinet door wouldn't stay shut. When the tiles got installed upside down and backwards.

Then there was the mystery surrounding the $5000 they'd advanced Danny for materials. Instead of showing up the next day with the receipts, as Janet had requested, he'd shown up a week later with a shiny red Chevy pick-up truck.

"How do you like my baby," Danny had stood there caressing one shiny fender. "Ol' Daniel's really comin' up in the world." He called himself Ol' Daniel when he was being especially folksy, or maybe especially dishonest.

Forget the receipts, Eric had said. Ol 'Daniel was a great guy, but he was no businessman. Cut Ol' Daniel some slack. Did it really matter anyway as long as Janet wound up with her big sage-green Jacuzzi tub in the end.

Only when the tub finally arrived it was white, and had two meager trickly jets instead of the six Janet had ordered. He'd gotten them a great price on it, Danny had said. He could paint it any color they liked—green, red, purple with polka dots. And those jets might look small, but they had tremendous power. You don't want more than two jets when you have power like that, he warned, or it'd blow your sweet ass right out of the water.

But Janet wasn't so blind she couldn't see what had happened. Ol' Daniel had substituted a bottom-of-the-line basic plain vanilla tub for the deluxe model she'd specified, and the difference, or the down payment on it anyway, sat in Ol' Daniel's driveway, gleaming from the hard wax Danny lovingly applied every weekend.

This was too much, Janet told Eric. He would have to confront Danny, demand an accounting. Impossible, Eric said. Trust was a sensitive issue with ex-cons, who were painfully aware of the stigma society attaches to felony convictions. In light of this, was it all that important that Janet be able to luxuriate in some oversized monstrosity of a bath fixture?

What could she say when he put it to her that way? But she wasn't happy.

A crummy too-small tub, Janet thought, the first time she attempted, unsuccessfully, to luxuriate in it. Crummy jets barely sufficient to carbonate the water. Crummy upside-down tiles on the wall opposite.

On the other hand, there was not one single crummy thing about Danny's red Chevy pick-up. She knew this because he'd proudly demonstrated each of its numerous options: the heated seats, the leather-covered steering wheel, the cup-holders, the mag wheels, the throbbing bass of the upgraded sound system, the metallic paint.

She drove a ten-year-old Toyota with wind-down windows.

And every time Janet considered that truck, she felt an unaccustomed fury stir within her, and she wanted to do terrible things.

The same fury she felt, sitting here now, waiting for the contractor who didn't show, who she knew in her heart would never show.

She was fifty years old. She'd given unstintingly to others, she reminded herself. To others who rarely appreciated it. To others who never paid her back. To others who took advantage of her too-soft heart, of her too-good nature.

She riffled through her stacks of paint samples until she found the shade she wanted. It was called 'shrieking violet,' and Ellie probably would have warned against it. Bright purple was hard, Ellie would have said. Bright purple was pretty near impossible.

Janet knew where he lived and that he parked the truck every night in the carport he'd built specially to shield it from the elements. It would be so easy. And he would never suspect her, not for a minute. He wouldn't suspect her even though she would paint purple flowers all over the truck, all upside down and sideways. Even though she would scratch a message on the hood: "Don't worry, I'll be back on Thursday to take care of it." He'd never suspect her because she knew she was invisible to him: middle-aged, small and harmless and decent to a fault.

Yes, sometimes even decency could be a fault, as Danny himself would have been the first to admit. She'd overheard Danny once, telling Eric how to survive in prison, Eric lapping it up, encouraging him. It's just like outside, Danny had said, people shitting on you until you start shitting on them. People fucking with you until you start fucking with them.

Janet tried not to see the world that way. How you saw the world, she believed, depended in part on where you chose to look. So when Janet read her morning paper, she found herself drawn to the back page stories of simple goodness—the couple that adopted severely handicapped children, the old woman who rescued wounded birds. In the retelling of folly and wickedness that constitutes the daily news, she was always searching for such manifestations of *Tikkun Olam*, of the repairing of the world. This is our obligation as Jews, as human beings, her grandfather the rabbi used to tell her—*Tikkun Olam*; to mend what is broken in the moral universe.

A broken world, Janet thought, as though the world were a house framed by some particularly inept Divine Contractor; by a God not unlike Danny perhaps, unable to get the cabinet doors to fit flush, or to install the tiles right side up. And so you lived, you good people, forever tightening the leaky faucets of evil with your little pocket wrenches of righteousness. Because if you didn't; if you and everybody like you stopped mending for even a day; if you relaxed and decided to watch television instead—maybe the whole structure would collapse all around you, around all of us, into the chaos, the dark nothing, the pure blank malevolence from which it came.

But still, Janet wondered, must you be repairing the world every single minute? Sometimes don't you get to do something—something wicked even—just for yourself?

Like shrieking violet. Done right—oh, done right, she imagined—it could be—it would be—oh, it will be—truly, truly elegant.

And so it was.

"If you want to understand what happened next," I said to Melissa Crane, (who was letting her hair grow out, until it now resembled a burgundy-tipped cactus), "remember that Janet had been doing nothing but good deeds practically her entire life. So once she'd had her first experience of mayhem, why she was like that convent girl who finally discovers sex...

There was no stopping her."

Chapter Seven
Janet Goes Wild

The eighteen-wheeler had been on her tail for ten minutes, honking, flashing its lights, making her so nervous she almost spilled her coffee.

Until he finally swerved into the right lane, rolled down his window and screamed:

"Move to Florida, why doncha. Drive a fucking golf cart."

Why did she always feel so humiliated, a little guilty even, when this happened? As if there were something wrong with *her* for obeying the posted speed limit? As if she had her nerve cluttering *his* personal highway?

But it also made her mad as Hell, and she wasn't going to take it anymore.

She followed him at a discreet distance until he pulled off into the parking lot of a forlorn roadside diner, a pale blue concrete box with one small pane of glass over the doorway. No one would be likely to spot her from inside, she thought, and the lot was almost deserted. Perfect conditions for what she had in mind.

Soon the driver emerged from the truck, and stuffed a giant garbage bag into an overflowing dumpster near the restaurant's entrance. The remains of a bucket o' chicken tumbled to the ground when he did this; also a root beer can which he kicked down the sloped walkway.

A litterer as well, it seemed. Janet wasn't surprised. It went together. The following-too-close. The littering.

Once he'd gone inside, she moved swiftly, stealthily, to the rig, and got to work. She had the whole operation down to two minutes flat by now.

A quick twist of the pencil. The air hissing out of the front tires. The note shoved under the wipers:

Tailgate THAT Asshole!
From the Slow and Careful Drivers
Liberation Front

Then she spray-painted a big purple flower on the hood.

Janet crouched in the shabby sedan, staking out the run-down house, waiting to confront the foul-mouthed punk who had rammed into her on his skateboard last week, and didn't even say, "I'm sorry." Sweat poured down her face. Maybe it was fear. More likely, she thought, a hot flash. For she was past fifty. Some people might think she should be sitting around discussing brow lifts. Or remodeling the kitchen. Doing something a little more age-appropriate anyway.

HA!!

She watched as he bounced out the door, him playfully shouting "suck my dick" to his neon-haired companion; the companion playfully rejoining, "suck mine c***s***er."

She raised the fake, but realistic looking, weapon.

This was going to be a real pleasure.

From the message board at Calltoflabbyarms.com

*Don't you just hate it: those young people you see everywhere nowadays, the ones whose vocabulary seems to consist entirely of the "F" word," F*** replacing every other part of speech as if it were some verb/noun/adjective-eating bacteria.*

I've had enough. Haven't you?

*Which is why I've developed the "F**k you!!, F**k you" product line, including my specially formulated licorice soap, for washing out potty-mouths. Harmless black dye stains teeth for 48 hours—really fun!*

It had been worth it, cultivating that contact in the Sheriff's Department, Jason thought. Lucky for him that he happened to have a real way with motherly file clerks.

He studied the surveillance tapes he'd sweet-talked her into copying for him—the ones from the restaurants and mini-marts where the vandal they'd nicknamed "The Purple Pimpernel" had struck.

There she was, the small thin woman in the hooded sweatshirt. Yes, when you looked closely, you could tell it definitely was a woman, though at first he had taken the shadowy figure for a teen-age boy.

He had spotted her three times, always somewhere in the background. The event itself never got captured on the tape, of course. She was much too clever for that. Still, there was a pattern here, but a pattern which might not have done Jason Wolf any good, if he hadn't happened to show the tapes to his cousin Craig, who'd been visiting from Las Vegas. Craig claimed he recognized her, that the woman looked exactly like his Remedial English teacher at Central Community College. Really nice lady, Craig had said. But that didn't eliminate her as a suspect, in Jason's book. The Queen Mum bandits had also been really nice ladies. They'd all been nice ladies. That's what made the whole thing so baffling.

It couldn't hurt to slip into one of this Dr. Miller's classes, Jason thought; pose as a student; take a quick snap with a camera phone; compare it to the tapes…

Who knew where it might lead? Just that morning he'd added another clipping to his collection:

From the *Contemporary Life* column: *Australia Today*

Bad dental care or bad manners?

Dateline: Sydney: Ebony teeth? Is this the latest teenage fad, or is it just another middle finger in the faces of mums and dads pushing those annoying annual checkups? Neither, says our youth style consultant, Ridley Ames. No one wants to talk about it, according to Ames, but over recent months, young people have found themselves the targets of what they're calling, "The F**k Police"—grannies in motorcycle jackets who surround the victim and wash his (or her) mouth out with a bad-tasting sludge, which leaves behind the telltale licorice-stained dentals that have become an increasingly familiar sight at local malls.

The seemingly well-coordinated campaign is definitely having an effect, states Ames. "I'm hardly ever hearing f**k anymore. It's all friggin this and friggin that, which," he winks, "is a f**king shame."

Janet huddled in the Chevy Caprice, sighting the trash-talking low-life through her whaddyacallem—crosshairs. She won't hurt him, she thought, just scare him a little, teach him some common courtesy. She wondered if she could hold out another ten minutes. Tried to remember how far back it had been to that Burger King she'd passed on the way. Or whether she should just head straight for the Texaco, even though they made you get a restroom key from the clerk there, and she didn't want to be remembered. Who was she kidding? As if the clerk would remember her. As if she'd be anything more to him than just another grey-haired woman with a bladder the size of a corn nut.

"Why is it," Janet Miller asked, "that all heroines have to be beautiful. Why can't the story ever begin, 'Once upon a time there was an average-looking Princess with a nice personality'?"

This always got a laugh out of the class, or one or two of the more thoughtful students, anyway. Rarely out of the men though, so she immediately took note of the new boy, the redhead, who chuckled appreciatively, and gave her a thumbs up.

"You don't believe me?" she said. "Here is my list of famous novels featuring a plain woman in a leading role."

She wrote on the blackboard in giant letters:

Jane Eyre

A few of the girls smiled, letting Janet know they "got it." Also the red-haired boy, who nodded rapidly, and scribbled in his notebook. Eager. It was a pleasure to see a student so eager, especially a male student, still—she didn't know what it was, but there seemed something a little over-eager, a little studied about him, as if he'd rehearsed his eagerness in front of a mirror that morning.

The smart girl, the one from Sri Lanka, raised her hand, and said in her soft lilting voice, enunciating each syllable.

"I think I know the point you are trying to make, Professor Miller, but I cannot see Count Vronsky throwing away his career for a just so-so Anna Karenina, no matter how agreeable she was, can you? Or Romeo committing suicide because he couldn't bear life without a Juliet who would be passable if not for the bad teeth."

Certainly she was much too smart for Janet's class. The other students exchanged looks whenever Kamalini raised her hand, which was often. It couldn't be easy for her socially, Janet thought, with her brains, her accent, her face like a boiled potato. Janet would like to have befriended her, encouraged her privately. And in the past, she might have done just that—met Kamalini for lunch in the cafeteria, recommended a few favorite modern authors, pushed her to go on to a good four-year college. But now Janet had no time, and other fish to fry.

She noticed the red-haired boy checking his cellphone. One of those text messages, she'd just bet. How rude they were nowadays, even the eager ones who laughed at your jokes.

She looked fondly at Kamalini, who probably had already come to the painful conclusion that she would never be the heroine of her own story. It wasn't fair. But then, Life isn't fair.

Janet surveyed the darkened street.

She'd had the strangest feeling lately, as if she were being followed. No, it wasn't just her imagination, she'd told the others, much less a guilty conscience. She kept noticing the same beat-up orange Volvo everywhere she went. It isn't every day you come across a "Dukakis for President" bumper sticker, so she knew it had to be the same one.

But she couldn't worry about that now. She needed to act quickly, before her quarry got away.

"Hey you," she yelled, "yeah, you."

They turned toward her, and saw the barrel of the gun poking through the rolled- down window.

"Fuck!" yelled the skateboarder.

"Fuckingmotherfuck," screeched his friend.

She pulled the trigger, relishing the feel of its cold metal against her finger; savoring the sibilant POP the weapon made as a cloud of green sulphurous slime burst from its barrel and covered the howling pair.

It would take days for the stink to dissipate, she laughed to herself; weeks for their skin to lose its sickly tint. They wouldn't forget her warning any time soon.

"Next time you run into someone, at least you could say I'm sorry," she shouted as she sped off, revving the motor. That would teach them.

Her exhilaration was short-lived.

She glanced in the rear view mirror. There it was again: the Volvo, and this time close enough that she could see the driver. He was young, very young, and his hair was a carroty red. She recognized him instantly.

"So Janet was The Purple Pimpernel?" Melissa shook her head, disbelieving," I never would've guessed."

"Well, Janet was the original Purple Pimpernel. As you know, there were copycats. Oh yes, the country was swarming with them at one time. And of all our accomplishments, I believe I am most proud of our role in restoring some measure of civility to the nation's highways.

"Of course, we paid a price, as you shall see. If only we had taken Janet more seriously when she told us she was being followed. Maybe we would have gotten wise to Jason Wolf earlier, and been more careful, and it might have turned out differently, even then.

"But we had been too busy with other things to worry about Janet,

things having to do with our personal lives.

"Carole had retired, and frequently was off traveling with Dennis to the many places she'd never been with Henry, such as Peru and Antarctica; and doing many of the things she'd never done with Henry, such as observing penguins in the wild, and trekking to Inca ruins.

"Ellie and Ramon were filming "Decayed Beauty," their prize-winning documentary celebrating the allure of the mature woman.

"As for me, I had a big decision to make, having to do with Mitch, who was finally divorced, and wanted to relocate to my city, and for us to move in together.

"I liked Mitch. Maybe I even loved Mitch. But the idea of sharing my cedar-lined closets with another human being had limited appeal. On the other hand, I liked Mitch; maybe I even loved Mitch, and I wasn't sure I wanted to grow old alone....

"So we were distracted, and that's how Jason Wolf was able to get those photos and blackmail us into getting involved...."

Melissa Crane turned on the machine.

"You mean involved in the...." she asked?

Yes. It was time to finally talk about the kidnapping. But how to begin? How to explain?

"I realize you may find this hard to believe, given what happened later," I said," but you must understand that people were always posting strange messages on the website, so when we saw that first one from Peppermint Patty, we didn't take it all that seriously. How could we? How could anyone? It had Big Fat Joke written all over it. Or so we thought..."

Book Four
The Kidnapping

Chapter Eight
Poetic Justice

From the message board at Calltoflabbyarms.com

Has this happened to anyone else? I'm a mother of four, grandma of seven, ten years passed the change, a good Christian, and suddenly I have this great big crush on somebody. Not only that. He's married. He lives in a different city. He's a Justice of the United States Supreme Court. I won't say which one. (Hint: dark, intense, a strict constructionist.)

Now I find myself reading his opinions in bed every night, which my husband, Charlie must think is strange, since I used to read books such as "Lust in the Swamp." But I quote to Charlie what you say on this web site, that us older ladies should explore new interests, such as Portuguese, or musical instruments or slashing tires (heh heh) and so forth. Not that Charlie understands much, him having the early-onset Alzheimers, which has been a challenge, but the Good Lord never gives us more than we can bear, aint that the truth.

Here's my problem. More and more, just reading Justice X's opinions isn't enough. I long to hear them from his own thin, pursed, bloodless, yet somehow oddly sensual lips. Now I'm having these fantasies about kidnapping him, and locking him up in my basement (not as bad as it sounds—it's finished, and there's a half bath). I would visit him every night, and we'd talk about everything under the sun, and especially the true intentions of the Founding Fathers regarding the Bill of Rights. He would be crazy about my three-cheese lasagna!

Should I just Go for It? You only Live Once!
Peppermint Patty from Pocatello

(Big Fat Joke, right? I mean—how many women reach middle-age and what they fantasize about is getting to listen to *more* of men's opinions?)

Six months later when he went missing, we thought at once of Peppermint Patty.

He had disappeared mysteriously from the hunting lodge in Montana where he went every year to shoot his annual elk —vanished into thin air—, and the talking heads began to speculate about kidnapping, or worse. After all, there were a lot of people who had good reason to hate Justice X, or even to wish him dead: environmental activists enraged by his vote to strike down the Endangered Species Act;[1] gay-rights activists enraged by his vote to uphold anti-sodomy laws;[2] radical feminists sick and tired of the way he always talked about the Founding Fathers, and never once mentioned the Founding Mothers. Round up the usual suspects.

Needless to say, suspicion didn't fall on a lovesick granny from Pocatello.

1. On the grounds that the Founding Fathers couldn't have intended to protect endangered species, since back then there were no endangered species—all of the species were doing just fine.
2. On the grounds that there was no evidence the Founding Fathers ever practiced sodomy, not even Ben "the wild and crazy father" Franklin.

I tried to imagine how she might have done it. She could have gotten hired as a housekeeper at the lodge, I supposed. She would have been dumpy, grey, innocuous. Even if someone happened to notice that she'd disappeared the same time as Justice X, it would have been called coincidence. A perfect crime by a perfect criminal: The Invisible Woman.

Still, we didn't feel any absolute obligation to come forward with our suspicions, which may be an indication of how far we'd already coasted down the slippery slope of moral relativism. Coasted, did I say—tobogganed, luged, tumbled headfirst.

"It's not as if we know for certain it was her," Ellie pointed out at dinner that night.

"But let's say it was," Carole joined in. "Would it hurt the man to learn some humility? Maybe he'll have more sympathy for the underdog after this."

"Instead of always siding with big corporations and against the working man and woman," Janet continued. "While as a general rule, I wouldn't endorse kidnapping, there may be times when a harmless little abduction is exactly what a person needs to build character."

I wasn't so sure.

Was I the only one who worried that Justice X might be in real danger? Who knew better than we did what homicidal rage can lie hidden beneath a grandmotherly facade? This is why I decided that if he didn't turn up in a couple of weeks, I would phone an anonymous tip to the authorities.

And I would have too, honestly I would have, if events hadn't forced my hand before that.

From the message board at Calltoflabbyarms.com

"Well sisters of the flabby arms, I've gone and done it. I prayed on it and prayed on it, and finally the Lord spoke to me saying, "God is Love," which I already knew, but it was nice to hear it from Jesus' own mouth. Jesus didn't mean carnal love, of course, which is from the Devil, so don't think that's why I did it, not for love of his body (which when you see it up close, without the robe, it's all kind of skinny and withered like Charlie's), but for love of his soul, which I hunger to join with mine, as the hart panteth after the stream.

Which has not happened yet, but I am patient and realize these things take time. Soon I will take the gag off his mouth (other than for eating), and we can talk, really talk, then he will understand that it was God's will, and maybe get past me having to use that gun, just a little one, not like the big rifle he shoots the elk with, which I think is wrong, the elk is also God's creature.

As far as Charlie getting suspicious goes, well, I never thought I'd say this, but Charlie coming down with the Alzheimers so young has turned out to be a real blessing in disguise. It is true the Lord works in mysterious ways. Charlie hears the noise coming from below, but he thinks it's 1952, and his daddy Big Charles is building a boat again, down the basement. I don't tell him any different. With Alzheimers sometimes it is best to just go along, that's what the visiting nurse used to say who I have told her not to come anymore, that Charlie is my responsibility and mine alone. She says I am a saint.

Tonight I think I will feed him (not Charlie, the other one) a special meatloaf with all the fixins. Anyone have a favorite recipe they'd like to share? He needs fattening up and is a picky eater.

He didn't know where he was (his *locus in quo*), or how she'd gotten him there (her *modus operandi*). All he remembered was that he'd fallen asleep at the lodge, fallen asleep easily and slept soundly, as he always did. Sometimes, especially after that business with Guitterez years back, strangers would scream at him in the street, "How do you manage to sleep at night?" What was their point? That he'd sent that degenerate to the gas chamber when it later turned out Guitterez was innocent, and someone else confessed to the crime. He slept at night because he knew that he'd done the right thing, even though it later turned out to be the wrong thing. What the screamers failed to understand was that just because you might be mistaken in the end didn't mean that you hadn't been correct in the first place.

Justice X considered himself a lucky man, sailing through life as he had on an unruffled sea of certitude. He credited this happy habit of mind in part to his deep religious faith, which had taught him to cling unwaveringly to fundamental principles, even in the face of overwhelming facts to the contrary. (He still secretly admired the Church for the tough stand it had taken on Copernicus.) Mainly though, he thanked his good genes. His father George had never been wrong either, and Justice X was a chip off the old block.

But right now, for the first time, he couldn't be certain of anything, not even where he was, much less how he'd gotten here.

He seemed to remember a sweet smell (chloroform?), something cold and steely poking his ribs. But even assuming she had drugged him, and abducted him at gunpoint—how had she managed to get past the armed guards who patrolled the roads to the lodge? And who was she anyway? She looked familiar. Then again, she looked like a million other women her age: overweight, with a round pleasant face, a droopy jawline, faded skin, thinning gray hair cut close to her head, thick bifocals. It was only when she removed the glasses and you saw the glittering eyes which never seemed to blink, the devouring eyes, that you would have said that there was anything unusual about her, anything that might have disqualified her from the position of Wal-Mart greeter, or school crossing guard, or other jobs suitable for elderly ladies.

She didn't speak much, and always with exaggerated respect, calling him, "Your Honor," which came across as a little sarcastic, given his situation. Nevertheless, she seemed to mean him no harm, unless you counted the meals—heavy, starchy concoctions which appeared three times a day, and were the only way he had of telling time. There were no windows in the place, and his watch had disappeared, so he marked the days (three of them he guessed, so far) thus: pancakes with bacon and sausage, bologna sandwich, lasagna (Day One). Jumbo omelette, corned beef hash, lasagna again, lemon meringue pie. (Day Two).

For the first day and a half he couldn't bear to touch the stuff. The smell of food nauseated him, mingling with the faint odor of mold and dust which permeated the room. Plus he suffered from a bad gallbladder, which could rack him with excruciating pain if he deviated from his usual bland, fat-free diet consisting of: plain oatmeal in the morning, a salad at noon, and for dinner, grilled fish and a baked potato, or brown rice.

She shook her head when she picked up his bright plastic meal trays, narrowed her lips and told him he had to eat, he must eat. She said this firmly, but with a certain maternal tenderness which he found more unnerving than any threat...

Back in his military days, he had sometimes wondered how he would hold up if he were ever captured by the enemy. There was little danger of this, him being assigned to the Judge Advocate General's staff, and rarely leaving the environs of Washington, DC. Still, he had enjoyed imagining his manly stoicism under torture, and the way he'd spit in his captor's face if the brute insulted the flag, etc.

But the captor of his youthful imaginings had been sly, Asian, implacably cruel, and never once asked whether he would care for maple syrup with his buttermilk waffles. Consequently, he was unprepared to find himself bound, gagged and force-fed by Grandma Moses, and was uncertain how to behave.

At first, he'd been imperious, demanding to know what he was doing there. He certainly hadn't "screamed," even though she had fluttered her plump hands and told him to stop "screaming" or he would wake some person named Charlie, who was not well. Then she put the gag back on, and he considered biting her, which he certainly would have done had she been sly, or implacably cruel, or at least male. But he couldn't bring himself to clamp his teeth around the thumb of a woman in a ruffled apron. He hadn't been raised that way. And what good would it have done anyway? She just would have gotten that same sorrowful, disappointed look she got when he told her he was lactose-intolerant and that's why he hadn't touched the lasagna with three kinds of cheese, her own secret recipe.

She left the gag off now, after he promised not to yell, (he didn't yell, only spoke with conviction), not that yelling would do him any good, she had informed him. The nearest neighbor was a quarter-mile away, and that was old Fred Coates who had seven German shepherds and couldn't hear a thing over the barking. Justice X deduced from this that he was being held in a rural area, and it might take longer for anyone to locate him than he had hoped.

Meanwhile he would have to find a way to placate the woman, which would be easier if he could figure out what she wanted. Not, he reassured himself again, nervously, that she seemed to mean him harm, though every once in a while, in between the tender looks and the hurt, disappointed looks, would come a flash of something deranged and dangerous. It was a look he'd seen in the eyes of criminals he had sentenced when he had been a trial court judge. Guitterez had had that look, and that's why it hadn't bothered Justice X that much that Guitterez had been put down like a mad dog, even though it turned out that Guitterez really had just been buying a carton of Marlboros at that convenience store, and hadn't shot the clerk in cold blood after all. Guitterez was a drug dealer, a thief with a three-pack-a-day habit, who probably would have died of lung cancer if he hadn't been executed first. If anything, Justice X had saved Guitterez from a slow painful death. Which goes to prove things were not always as cut and dried, morally speaking, as Justice X's critics liked to pretend.

By corned-beef-hash day he had talked her into leaving the ropes off his hands, explaining about his prostate problem, and how he sometimes needed to use the restroom in between her visits, when she would unbind his wrists and wave him shyly toward the half-bath with the fuzzy pink rug. She had blushed and frowned, then said Charlie had the same problem; only because Charlie also had the Alzheimer's, he sometimes forgot he had the problem, and made a mess. Which is why she had him in adult diapers now. For a minute there Justice X thought the crazy woman was about to make him the same offer, which horrified him more than the prospect of having his fingernails pulled out with pliers, or the soles of his feet beaten with a rubber baton, or anything else the imaginary Colonel Tranh or Major Matsushita could have dreamed of to extract information beyond name, rank and serial number.

Instead, she removed the ropes, which was exactly what he'd wanted. Now that his hands were free, he figured it shouldn't be all that difficult to escape. Only a bolted iron gate blocked the stairs to the upper story and freedom. He could overpower her, even shackled by the ankles as he was. Then he would lock the door behind him, sit his way up the stairs and get to a telephone...

It couldn't happen soon enough. If the food didn't kill him, the boredom might.

By day two, he was so hungry he'd wolfed down the lemon meringue pie, the least offensive offering on his tray. The pie had been delicious, the best thing he'd tasted in a long time, welcome relief both from starvation and from the flavorless virtue of his regular diet. He ate the pancakes the next morning too, drowned in butter and honey, and was surprised when the only effect on his gastrointestinal tract was a not unpleasant sensation of fullness.

Feeding his mind was not so easy. The entertainment on offer consisted of a Bible, a deck of well-thumbed pinochle cards, and a television set which only got three channels through the twisted coat hanger which served as an antenna. She apologized that she had been forced to cancel the Satellite service just before Justice X became her "guest," but it seemed they were barely making it on Charlie's disability pension as it was, and the doctor had given Charlie a prescription for this new drug which cost as much as their car payment. Aha! Ransom then. Was she after money? Name her price, he'd said, and immediately regretted it because her eyes got that mad dog look, and she held up her hands as though he'd struck her. How could he think that? Then it burst out of her. She loved him. Loved him.

Oh God, it was worse than he had thought.

He tried not to imagine what she might have in mind; he only knew he had to act soon, before she overcame her natural female reticence. He would rush her when she brought dinner that night, he decided, or maybe right after dinner. She had promised meatloaf and mashed potatoes, with double fudge chocolate cake for dessert, and his mouth watered just thinking about it. He couldn't believe his appetite, nor explain why his intestines weren't tied in knots all the time, the way they were at home.

She set the tray down on the collapsible table, and sat beaming as she watched him gobble up everything on his plate, even the broccoli. As he'd planned, he asked for seconds on dessert, and when she turned around to go, he swiveled up from his seat and threw the whole force of his body against her, knocking her to the floor. He grabbed the key from the pocket of her apron and began to scuttle towards the gate as fast as his shackled legs would allow, and he was almost there when he felt a hand grip his ankle, and then the terrible pain in his thigh and the voltage shooting through him. And then everything went dark.

From the Calltoflabbyarms message board

Sisters: I have done something I am not proud of, and need your help and support and yes your forgiveness. If you can find it in your hearts, which Jesus already has, I know because he told me! But not everybody is the son of God, sent to save us from our sins, so you may find it a little harder. Even though hopefully some of you have found yourself in a similar situation, and will understand. It could happen to anybody! You carry something to protect yourself in case you are attacked by an intruder (out here all alone in the country), and instead, somehow you use it on a person you love and respect, maybe one of the great men of the age!

Now how can I ever restore the trust that was beginning to grow between us? Question? Can a relationship survive a thousand volts from a stun gun? I could kick myself. Just when things were going so well. Oh and Birmingham Belle—thanks for your prize-winning double chocolate fudge cake. It's like you said. Everybody will ask for seconds.

P. Patty

Well you might have thought someone would have noticed and turned Patty in, but the thing is, like I told you, women were always posting their fantasies on the message board, some of them even creepier than this, so it's not really surprising that only one person took it seriously. And he had no business lurking around our website in the first place. There oughta be a law…

"Any lunatic can put anything on the Internet. Isn't that supposed to be the whole beauty of it?"

I tossed the sheaf of papers back at Jason Wolf. He had printed out every message Peppermint Patty had posted on Calltoflabbyarms.com, including her recipe for salmon croquettes. They added up to something, he insisted, and he was going to Pocatello to check it out. This story had Pulitzer Prize written all over it.

And Jason was here in my office to invite me along, me and my friends. Because we would understand the woman's psychology. Know how to talk to her. If this Peppermint Patty did have Justice X in her basement, the way she claimed, another woman might be able to convince her to let him go, without the police getting involved, and spoiling the ending Jason had in mind, which featured Jason Wolf in the role of Hero, and no gunplay.

"Are you out of your mind?" I said, "Why on earth would we want to schlep to Poca-wherever-it-is on some fool's errand?"

He didn't reply. Instead he splayed some photographs across my desk.

I studied the pictures. There was Janet Miller committing all those little felonies which had been so amusing at the time, but now, it appeared, could put her behind bars for quite a few years. And, it seemed, he'd followed the rest of us too.

Taken pictures of us at our Wednesday night dinners; our girls' nights out at the movies, our own tire slashings….

Damn Jason Wolf. Damn him to Hell.

The first thing Justice X saw when he came to was her weeping face hovering over him, and the first thing he heard was her babbling something about how sorry she was that she'd ever taken that women's self-defense class at the Community Center, because she had reacted instinctively when he pushed her down. Could he ever forgive her?

Let him go he said, and he'd consider it, though of course he wouldn't. He would never forgive her. He would see to it that she was prosecuted to the full extent of the law; beyond the full extent of the law, if possible—to the full extent of the law as dispensed in Texas or Alabama.

She shook her head. She couldn't let him go. Anything but that.

So much for remorse, Justice X thought, and considered how else he might persuade and manipulate this strange woman to his will. No use. His mind was blank. It had been 35 years since the last time he'd had to ingratiate himself with another person, back when he'd courted Doris, and he seemed to have forgotten how it was done. Browbeat. Command. Overbear. Intimidate. This he understood, and it had always been enough…until now. Suddenly he felt very tired, and couldn't think of anything to do except to ask, with infinite weariness:

"What do you want? Just tell me what you want."

She reached out and patted his bald head with a napkin, as

though she were drying a lettuce.

"Tomorrow, after dinner," she smiled, "I'm making my special chicken stew with butter dumplings. Homemade cherry cobbler for dessert."

He couldn't help himself. Furious as he was, his mouth watered just thinking about it.

Special Agent Kim Kozlowski studied the police artist's drawing of the woman who had called herself Alice Adams, then tossed it back on the desk.

"She could be anybody. She could be my mother-in-law."

Lt. Mike Walsh, Glacier County Sheriff's Department, chewed his thumbnail, or what was left of his thumbnail, which he'd bitten to the bloody quick since Justice X had disappeared from Blackfoot Lodge. Between the television crews camped in front of his office, and SpecialAgentSuperBitch here letting him know every way possible that she considered him an incompetent rube, Sheriff Walsh was a nervous wreck. He needed to go somewhere and let off steam, get drunk, take the life of a large mammal. Fuck's chance of that, he knew, until the judge was found, dead or alive, Walsh was thinking probably dead at this point. It had been a week, and in the Sheriff's experience, unless you were talking teenage runaways, a week generally meant dead. He didn't see much point in chasing after this Alice Adams or whoever she was, but there was even less point in trying to talk sense to a representative of the federal government.

"We couldn't get a good description," he said. An understatement. Older lady. Gray hair. Overweight. Nice.

"I guess we'll give it to the press anyway, for what it's worth," Kozlowski sighed." It's all we've got to go on right now."

The other employees at the lodge had alibis which checked out, leaving only this part-time housekeeper who had vanished as mysteriously as the judge. Alice Adams wasn't her real name, and the address she'd given in Kalispell wasn't a real address, and her Social Security number was pure fiction. Suspicious circumstances, in Kozlowski's book, even if that yokel of a sheriff couldn't see it.

The judge's disappearance was getting to be a major embarrassment for the Bureau, and especially for Kozlowski, the agent-in-charge. She suspected that that's why she'd been made the agent-in-charge, in fact. She'd risen too far too fast for the comfort of a lot of the Old Boys, and now they were setting her up for a fall...

The phone rang—her mother-in-law calling to say she'd found something on the internet Kozlowski really ought to take a look at.

Kozlowski wrote down the name of the website. She'd check it out, just to humor Cecile (who had way too much time on her hands now that she'd retired), though it was a well-known fact that any lunatic could post anything on the Internet. And what self-respecting criminal mastermind would go by a name like Peppermint Patty?

"Superb," he said, wiping the last traces of the chicken

stew from his thin mustache, "absolutely superb."

Absolutely superb might be an exaggeration, but the dish certainly qualified as "tasty," and the biscuits were especially impressive—small marvels of creamy fluffiness. He'd eaten five, and had stopped only when she gently reminded him to leave room for dessert. "Sure got an appetite, bless your soul," she had laughed and he'd smiled back. Sure, he was still extremely upset with her for kidnapping him, tying him up, practically electrocuting him etc. But ever since he'd stumbled on that box, he couldn't help also liking her, just a little.

She had unshackled his legs that morning, leaving him free to explore his pine-paneled prison, all 15 by 20 paces of it, not that there was much to see: a souvenir spoon collection; a homemade magazine rack containing three-year-old TV Guides; numerous framed photographs of indistinguishable blond children posed stiffly against studio backgrounds representing "The Beach" or "Autumn Woods."

Then he discovered it, stuffed on the top shelf of a closet filled with neatly labeled cartons: " Baby clothes" (Jennifer); "Art work" (Casey); "Crochet Patterns" (Afghans-Booties). This particular crate, however, had no label other than the stick-on hearts plastered along the sides. He opened the thing, without much interest, expecting to find, maybe, "Valentine's Day cards" (1992).

Instead, meticulously alphabetized and tied in pink satin ribbon, there were all of Justice X's opinions since he'd been named to the high bench. And underneath these, a scrapbook of newspaper clippings, and an 8 x 10 glossy of Justice X in his robe, his face covered with bright red lipstick kisses.

He'd stood there, transfixed. He knew he had admirers, of

course, who wrote misspelled letters praising him for upholding traditional American values. He had disciples. He had sycophants. But never in his wildest dreams had he imagined that he had a Fan—a crazed fan at that—and he had to admit, the idea tickled him. For all that he disapproved of rock stars in principle, he didn't mind being a little bit of one, any more than the next man.

So he wasn't totally unprepared that evening when, after clearing away the dinner dishes, she pulled *Lawrence versus City of Jacksonville* out of her apron pocket and whispered huskily, "Please, could you explain what you meant here where you wrote 'if the Founding Fathers had intended to enshrine a right to buggery in the Constitution, they would've put it in there along with the right to bear arms.'"

And he had.

Sisters of the flabby arms:

It really is like a dream come true! Sometimes I have to pinch myself. Everything just the way I pictured except he can't eat my lasagna on account of he is lactose intolerant. Even their, he is sorry because he knows if he could eat it he would love it, the same way he loves all my good cookin'! He's gained 10 pounds since I took him in and believe me he needed it. The man was a walking skeleton because I bet his wife, that Doris, is one of those spoiled rich biches (pardon my french) who is always off getting her toenails painted. For instance, every morning, he had nothing but instant oatmeal for breakfast, CAN YOU BELIEVE IT *and he had to make it himself besides.*

Now every night after I give Charlie the sleeping pill, I go downstairs and he (the other one) reads to me for as long as his voice holds out. His throat is not very strong so I said it was okay if he skips the boring parts—he says they are called "procedural issues"—and gets straight to where the court is making a travesty of the Constitution, and James Madison is spinning in his grave, which he points out in all of his opinions, which he calls "blistering dissents."

We are getting along so good I even made a joke last night about how poor Mr. Madison's shroud must be pretty near worn out from all that whirling around in the coffin, but he didn't think it was funny; he doesn't have much of a sense of humor, especially when it comes to himself. But he is a Great Man and so I guess he doesn't need one.

Now he is pestering me to call that Doris and let her know that he is all right, she must be worried. Well she should of thought of that and been a real wife who made her husband a hot breakfast instead of running off to the beauty parlor all day long, and maybe he would have stayed with her in the first place.

Oh and BubbeJill—tried the rum with honey and lemon, and you were right. It works great for larinjitis.

P. Patty

Jason Wolf brushed his teeth, getting ready for bed though it was only just past 11 PM. He'd barely slept the night before, and had been on his feet all day, canvassing every church in Pocatello to hand out flyers about a new Christ-centered Alzheimer's support group.

Time well spent. He hadn't gotten very far with the Episcopalians or Methodists, who immediately demanded to see his credentials. Or with the Unitarian minister, who explained that they didn't go in much for Christ-centered anything except on major holidays.

From the Evangelicals though, he soon had a list of two dozen folks this could be a real blessing for, Praise the Lord.

Things had gone almost *too* well with the Evangelicals, Jason thought. It bothered him that he had managed to pass himself off so easily as a true Bible-believing Christian, when his entire disguise consisted of a "My Boss is a Jewish Carpenter" T-shirt. It bothered him because Jason had a great big secret. Which was that, despite his best efforts, and a couple of near misses, Jason still was a technical virgin, and worried constantly that it showed. Why else, he now fretted, would the folks at Calvary Foursquare Gospel Church have accepted him as one of their own, no questions asked, unless it showed? He stared at his reflection in the speckled mirror over the motel sink, checking out the dark, (world weary?) circles under his eyes. Yes!, he told himself, maybe they'd taken him for a reformed sinner, a guy who'd been sinning on a regular basis since he was, like, 14 years old, and that's how come they'd welcomed him right off. He'd read somewhere that there was nothing God loved like a *reformed* sinner, and the same could very well be true of Pastor Gormley, who'd slipped Jason five names and a fifty-dollar contribution for the Lord's work.

He put on his blue-striped flannel pajamas, sat cross-legged on the lumpy mattress and studied the list of Christian Alzheimer's victims, now down to four, after he'd crossed off all the women and the nine men who were in nursing homes. He circled the most promising prospect, the one named Charles—Charles Eveready, who lived with his wife Margaret on a ranch 15 miles outside of town. Attorney

Stern and the others would be arriving in Pocatello tomorrow morning. Maybe they'd all just take a ride out to the Eveready spread and reconnoiter; pose as the Calvary Foursquare Gospel Church Helping Hands committee; bring along a tuna casserole. Whatever. He'd think of something.

Big Day ahead of him, maybe the biggest of his young life. He set the alarm for 8 A.M., snuggled under the covers, hugged his fuzzy old pooh bear, and 15 minutes later was out cold, dreaming of hot naked babes.

It's like riding a bicycle, Justice X reflected; you never really forget how. Many years ago, when he was a new-minted lawyer, he'd had to curry favor, to kiss up, to ingratiate himself the same as any other young man on the make. Now he reached back into the toolbox of memory to retrieve the dimly recollected skills, grown rusty from disuse.

Flattery: Praise her cooking. The biscuits are exquisite. What is the secret spice you put in the marinated lamb shanks? Admire her grandchildren. Cute as buttons. Compliment her new haircut.

Be interested in her sad, boring life. Her drooling husband. Her son Casey, who lived far away and rarely called and might be homosexual. The bankruptcy two years ago after Charlie invested in one of those get-rich-quick schemes, which actually turned out to be a get-broke-quick scheme, and lost their life savings. Her diabetes and high blood pressure. Her grandson's learning disability.

Pretend to enjoy her company: Tell her how refreshing

it is to be around somebody so down-to-earth, instead of those fancy Washington types with their cocktail parties and hundred-dollar words. Disparage Doris, however disloyal this made him feel.

In short, lull her into believing there was nothing Justice X would rather do than spend the rest of his days in her basement, downing her food, basking in her adoration.

Then make his move.

The truly frightening part was that he actually was beginning to half-enjoy himself; that he was only *half* pretending to be interested in her life; only *half* faking pleasure in her company. This evening, for instance, when he was reading to her from *Scott v Berg*, and she clapped her mottled hands like a little girl, and shouted, "Hooray, you tell em!," he caught himself thinking: if you had to be abducted at gunpoint by a maniac, it probably didn't get much better than this. Plus he couldn't remember the last time he'd felt so relaxed. Gone the twisting knife in his gut. Gone the constant headache behind his right temple. He wondered if the woman was slipping something into his food, some chemical that would cause him eventually to morph into a big happy baby like the one upstairs, lolling around in his diapers, imagining it's 1952.

Escape! He had to escape before it was too late!

But first, he could use some more of that cherry cobbler. He rang the buzzer she'd given him. Plenty of time to put his plan into action tomorrow, after breakfast. Eggs Benedict. Yum.

Kim Kozlowski had never felt at ease around the clergy.

Something about them—as if they had x-ray vision into your soul. As if they could tell, just by looking, that you cheated on your income tax, and had once had a fling with a married cop from Milwaukee.

She especially didn't feel at ease around this Gormley person. Maybe it was his high-pitched asthmatic voice, or the fact that he resembled the Pillsbury doughboy. Even the hand he'd offered her to shake had felt sticky and warm, like a bun fresh from the oven. Sometimes the clergy made her skin crawl, and this definitely was the case with Reverend Augustus Gormley, of the Calvary Foursquare Gospel church.

He crossed his puffy arms over his pouter pigeon chest, body language Kozlowsi read as, "you're not getting dick out of me." Just as well. She was wasting her time here, and God she was tired; couldn't wait to get back to the motel and soak her weary body in the chipped tub, toss in some of the strawberry bubble bath she always brought along on business trips. Maybe take a nip from the bottle of Johnny Black she also brought along.

But the instant she mentioned Justice X, Gormley's entire attitude seemed to change. His sausage arms flew out embracing the air, and his voice rose an octave.

"One of the great men of our times." he squeaked, "a tremendous loss, a tragedy for the entire country."

Turned out Gormley was a huge fan of Justice X, "a man of God on a Court of heathens." He gave sermons about him. He'd organized the Foursquare Gospel Church Justice X study group, with the help of Sister Margaret Eveready, bless her soul. Of course, Sister Margaret didn't attend much anymore since her husband Charlie had gotten so bad with the Alzheimer's;

sometimes so bad she had to put him in a nursing home for a week, just to get some rest…

Kozlowski was wide-awake now, as awake as she'd ever been in her entire 37 years. Could it be? A Charlie with Alzheimer's? An unexplained absence when Sister Margaret could have become Alice Adams, part-time housekeeper at Blackfoot Lodge? What if Justice X were being held captive on the Eveready Ranch even as they spoke? What if she went out there and rescued him all by herself? Sure, Official Policy said she should call for backup in this situation. Fuck Policy. If she couldn't handle Old Lady Eveready on her own, without backup, she didn't deserve her badge, much less to even think about becoming the very first female director of the Federal Bureau of Investigation before her fortieth birthday.

He sneezed. Then sneezed again. He had inhaled a pinch of ground pepper saved from lunch, but she didn't know that.

She handed him a lace-trimmed handkerchief.

"You're not coming down with anything, are you?" she asked, anxiously, " I can make you my special eucalyptus chest rub."

Her unsuspecting innocence made his heart lurch. She wasn't a bad woman, not really, only crazy as a loon, three Pepsis short of a six-pack, an amendment shy of the Bill of Rights. And yet, for all her limitations, she still was capable of appreciating the finer points of his jurisprudence—better than Doris did actually. A shame, in a way, that Margaret would have to spend the rest of her life in prison....

"It's something in the air down here," he coughed, rubbing at his watery eyes.

She shook her head.

"Mold. You can't get rid of it in a basement, not even with bleach. I know. My Casey also could be hypersensitive to mold."

He coughed harder, shoulders heaving. He didn't much like being lumped in with a suspected homosexual, a homosexual with allergies, but if that's what it took...

"If only," he gasped, "I could get some fresh air..."

"Fresh air?" her voice trembled, "You want fresh air?" The frown lines on her forehead deepened as she considered the implications. She was cunning, for all her simplicity, the Judge thought, and he must play his part with great care. "But if I let you out, you might run away," she said slowly. "And then I would be all lonesome again."

"Run away?" He touched her wrist. Her skin felt like dead moths. "Why would I run away? What more could a man want than good food and the company of a good woman?"

He'd picked up that line from one of the soap operas he now watched every afternoon—a line used with great success by one Vinnie DeLuca, who married unattractive widows, and promptly disappeared with their bank accounts. Obviously, it was the kind of thing women wanted to believe, and so they did.

Margaret wanted to believe it. He could tell by the way she bit her narrow lips. He knew all her expressions by now, all half-dozen or so. Maybe that's all she needed in her uncomplicated life.

"I suppose I could tie you to me with a rope," she said at last, "so if you ran away, you'd have to take me along."

Justice X tried to imagine Doris' reaction if he arrived home in Chevy Chase dragging Margaret behind like a piece of rolling luggage. The idea tickled him. While he disapproved of harems in principle, he realized he wouldn't mind having a little bit of one, any more than the next man. Of course Doris would never go for it. She was the most conventional woman he'd ever met. That had been part of the attraction way back when. Now he wondered if he might have been happier if he'd been a little more adventuresome in that department.

"Naturally," he said, "if it would make you feel secure."

The important thing was to get outside. Then he would figure out how to deal with the rope. In fact, the rope might come in handy. He could use it to tie her up while he ran for help, to that neighbor with the dogs…

"I'll be back in a jiffy," Margaret said. Her face brightened. "Why don't I bring along a picnic? Some of the leftover roast beef with horseradish sauce, a nice French potato salad, and half a blueberry pie. How does that sound?"

Yes—he definitely would miss Margaret's cooking. Maybe he could pull strings to get her into some special penitentiary-based catering program which offered home delivery. True, Justice X always had vigorously opposed vocational training or other frills in the prison system. Now he wondered if he'd been shortsighted. Not wrong, exactly, just not 100% right.

She was already upstairs when he heard the car, and then the doorbell, ringing, ringing.

"What a dump," Kozlowski thought, peering through her

binoculars. The crumbling old farmhouse reminded her of her Great-aunt Agnes' place in Wisconsin, where Kozlowski had been forced to spend one summer vacation when she was in grade school. It'll be good for you to get out of the city, her mother had said, breathe some fresh country air. That was about all there had been to do at Aunt Agnes'—breathe the air and feed the two scrawny chickens which pecked at your legs when you weren't looking. The whole experience had left Kozlowski with a permanent distaste for everything rural.

She couldn't imagine why anyone deliberately would choose to live way out here where you couldn't even get a pizza delivered. And according to Gormley, the Evereadys had been doing it for generations, ever since Great Grandpa Zeke or whoever—Koslowski had stopped listening by then—had homesteaded the place back in the 1880s.

Geez. No wonder Margaret Eveready went off the deep end and kidnapped a Supreme Court Justice. Probably desperate for the company.

Poor woman. If Kozlowski herself were going to kidnap someone for company, Justice X would have been about her last choice. She studied the picture of him she'd brought along. The man looked about as entertaining as a root canal.

Two hours she'd been sitting here watching. Zip. Zero. Nada. Not a sign of life. Not a sound except for the flies buzzing around a shitpile. She didn't know how much longer she could stay hidden in the bushes waiting for the woman to leave, so Kozlowski could go in and snoop around for Justice X. Policy would have said, "get a warrant." Fuck Policy. First off, she didn't have enough evidence for a warrant. A message posted on a website? You couldn't bust a meth lab on that kind of evidence, much less a nice old church lady. Sure, Kozlowski knew in her gut that Justice X was in there. But she doubted her gut would be enough to convince a judge to sign a warrant, not even in Idaho, where they weren't all that particular about these things.

She heard the car before she saw it.

It sounded big and powerful, and left swirling brown dust devils behind. She raised the binoculars. The thing looked like something you'd drive to a funeral. Fuck her Luck. Maybe she was already too late.

Carole gritted her teeth.

"OK, raise your hand if you really believe that the only vehicle they had left at the Pocatello Thrifty was a Lincoln Town Car?"

"I told you, you should have dressed more country," Jason said. "They saw you coming a mile away."

She eased the behemoth down the bumpy gravel road leading to the Eveready spread. The rental company had been very emphatic about the matter of pebbles dinging the fenders, and she was being extra cautious, even for Carole.

Sometime this year, I thought. Justice X could die of old age by the time we got there.

I had about made up my mind to get out and walk, when the farmhouse appeared around what turned out to be the final bend. It was a foreboding sight—three stories high, with peeling acid green paint, and decrepit screens nibbled by the resident rodents.

We sat quietly, studying the place. You could imagine weary travelers finding refuge here in a storm, only to find themselves chopped up for breakfast sausage. Nobody seemed to be in a big hurry to get out of the car.

"Well," Jason said at last, "if we're going to do it, I guess we should do it."

Ellie shuddered and picked up the casserole dish. I grabbed the flowers, while Janet took the mylar balloon bouquet out of the trunk.

We walked to the door, huddling close together. I pressed what was left of the bell, which appeared to have been gnawed at by something, possibly the same something which had done in the screens.

Soon we heard light footsteps approaching, and could sense, rather than see, an eye peering through the peephole. Then we heard the footsteps rapidly retreating before we could even wave the balloons and shout, "Helping Hands Committee!"

Then we heard something else—a cry, almost a wail, coming from somewhere deep inside the house.

"Did you hear that, "Jason whispered, his voice trembling. "He's in there; I know it." He shoved his shoulder against the locked door, which didn't budge.

"Don't be an idiot," I pulled him back. "She has a gun and a taser and she doesn't hesitate to use them."

Our cellphones were useless out there. And while Jason wasn't happy about the idea of us driving to the neighbor's house and calling the cops, he liked the idea of being alone on the Eveready spread even less.

We were about halfway back up the access road when

we heard the shout in the distance: "Freeze! Police," turned around and drove back.

He knew he was taking a risk, trying to get the attention of whoever was at the door. But these were the first visitors to show up since Margaret had brought him here, nearly—what—two weeks ago, and he at least had to try. The sound of the bell seemed to have awakened him from a kind of trance, and he remembered who he was—Justice X, admired, feared, one of the dominant legal minds of his generation. It's like Circe and the pigs, he thought, meaning Circe, the sorceress who plied Odysseus' men with food and drink and turned them into swine. So it was with him and Margaret in her basement, him slowly reverting to a primal oinkiness, dreaming of his slop, looking forward to that day's installment of "As the World Turns." How thin is the veneer of civilization, he shuddered, how easily lost.

"Help!" he screamed, "Help!"

He had no idea how far away the front door was, or how well sound traveled in this house she had once described as a "big drafty old thing." He yelled louder, more desperately.

No response except for the echo of his own voice. The visitors seemed to have left, and he heard Margaret thumping down the stairs. He rubbed the spot on his leg where she had stunned him. The woman could be so unpredictable…

He knew he had to think fast, and act even faster. Maybe fake a heart attack. He'd seen one just yesterday on that hospital show which came on at four o'clock. How did it go?

Arghh, he groaned, collapsing to the floor, clutching his breast.

In an instant she was kneeling at his side, pressing her chapped lips to his mouth, pumping his chest way too hard with her sturdy little hands. She smelled like lilacs.

Kozlowski studied them through her binoculars as they got in their big car and drove away. The boy, the one in the cowboy-style leisure suit, kept looking back out the window, as if he'd left something behind.

Who were they, she wondered, and what were they doing here? Kozlowski had just about made up her mind to hike back to where she'd hidden her own car and follow them —they were driving that slow—when a small stocky woman staggered out of the house, leading a tall man by a rope tied around his waist.

Kozlowski recognized him immediately -- the judge himself, alive, and if not kicking, at least stumbling.

"Freeze! Police!" she hollered, bursting from the shrubbery, weapon cocked. What a rush! Kozlowski had been wanting to yell Freeze! Police! ever since she'd joined the Bureau, but had never come even close to having a chance before. First she got stuck in mail fraud where, if you were lucky, you got to yell, "drop the envelope—NOW." Then she got transferred to some crappy desk job with a fancy title, and finally the promotion six months ago after that congresswoman started making noises about gender equity. Freeze!, she hollered again, just to hear herself say it, loving the way it exploded out of her throat like when you pop the cork on a bottle of champagne.

Maybe she overdid it, this being her first time, because Margaret Eveready froze all right. Beyond froze. She crumpled to the ground, and the judge crumpled right on top of her.

"Don't shoot her," the man cried, holding up his hands, in the classic posture of surrender, "It's me I think you're looking for."

He untied the rope and lurched toward Kozlowski, shading his eyes as though the light pained him.

Kozlowski approached slowly, keeping her weapon trained on Margaret Eveready. No sense taking any chances. The perp might appear harmless at the moment, even dead at the moment, but she knew that this Margaret, a.k.a. Alice Adams a.k.a. Peppermint Patty, was also capable of electrocuting you if you rubbed her the wrong way.

"I think she might need medical attention," Justice X reached out and blindly grabbed Kozlowski's arm. "She suffers from high blood pressure, and is borderline diabetic."

Jesus Christ, what did he expect Kozlowski to do about it? Margaret Eveready shoulda considered her health before she embarked on a life of crime. Like lacrosse, kidnapping is a young man's game. Now Kozlowski had to figure out how to carry the two of them to her vehicle, seeing as how Margaret was practically dead, and His Honor could barely walk.

That's when she heard the big car creeping back down the road.

"Freeze!" she yelled again, just to hear herself say it.

A strange sight met our eyes as we approached the house —a

large, mannish woman brandishing a revolver, and a few yards away, a thin man kneeling over someone, administering CPR.

"I'm gonna require that car," the woman barked, introducing herself as Kim Kozlowski, Special Agent, Federal Bureau of Investigation. She had a square head, with the features clustered in the center like a lonely village on an empty plain, and straight dishwater blonde hair pulled back in a ponytail so tight it made me wince.

"She's not dead is she?" Jason looked as if he were about to throw up. "Did you have to shoot her?"

"Of course I didn't shoot her," Kozlowski boomed. "I just yelled at the woman. How was I supposed to know the perp would go all coronary on me?"

The man shook his fist.

"No. She's not dead, no thanks to you Agent Kozlowski, but we've got to get her to a hospital immediately," he shouted.

I recognized him from his picture. Actually, he looked better than his picture, more relaxed. And he'd filled out. His face, for instance, no longer resembled something you might stick on a warning label for hazardous chemicals. The Judge's two-week stay in Margaret Eveready's basement seemed to have done him good.

"Justice X, I presume," Jason oozed. "I am so thrilled to meet you, I've been a great admirer…." (Not exactly. Jason's code name for the Judge was " Justice Cave-Dweller.")

"Yes, yes," the man interrupted, ignoring Jason's outstretched hand. "I'm Justice X. And who the hell are you?"

"Yeah, who the hell are you?" Kozlowski scanned our faces as if she were trying to remember whether she'd seen them displayed at the post office recently. "And what the f...Sam Hill are you doing out here?"

Kozlowski looked from one to the other of us, and beetled her scanty brows. I shuffled my feet. She had this way of making you feel guilty, even though you hadn't done anything wrong yet, not really. It's a skill they must teach at Authority Figure U.

Damn Jason, and his damn Pulitzer Prize.

Even now, he couldn't pass up an opportunity for a scoop, shoving his tape recorder in the Judge's face.

"How does it feel to be rescued after two weeks in captivity, Your Honor? Is there anything you'd like to say to the people of America now that your long ordeal is over?"

Unfortunately for Jason's ambitions, what His Honor had to say would be unprintable in a family newspaper, involving as it did Jason performing certain anatomically impossible acts. Then His Honor abruptly terminated the interview by grabbing the tape recorder and lobbing it at the nearest tree.

"This woman is dying," he thundered, "you moron, and you want to know how I feel?" The judge spit the "feel" out of his mouth as if it were a piece of gristle.

He bent down and shook Margaret Eveready, then kissed her wrinkled forehead. When he looked up, I could see the tears pooling at the corners of his hard eyes.

"She wasn't a bad woman," he whispered, "not really, just —troubled. But she—she truly appreciated my jurisprudence, and her chicken with butter dumplings—pure heaven."

His proud head sagged. Even Jason knew enough to keep his big mouth shut.

Epilogue:

"Stockholm syndrome," the pundits called it.

The well-documented psychological phenomenon where the captive begins to identify with the captor; the prisoner with the guard.

How else to explain Justice X's bizarre behavior, refusing to press charges against Margaret Eveready, who, as it turned out, had merely fainted, and revived almost as soon as we got her into the car. The judge himself wouldn't talk about it, except to say that Mrs. Eveready was mentally ill and deserved sympathy, not punishment, a position which only went against everything he had stood for his entire life.

So naturally the wild theories began flying around the Internet. Such as the real Justice X had been murdered, and this liberal impostor substituted in his place. Proof: the fake "Justice X" was at least ten pounds heavier than the "real" Justice X, and had been spotted at a Kentucky Fried Chicken drive-up window, when everybody knew the real Justice X had an iffy gallbladder, and even a two-piece mini meal could land him in the emergency room.

—Margaret never did go to prison. She and Charlie took up residence at an expensive sanitarium instead, financed by the undisclosed sum a British tabloid paid for the exclusive rights to Margaret's story. There are rumors that a certain tall man visits her there once a month, and comes away loaded down with Tupperware containers, which he returns clean and empty.

—Jason parlayed his riveting first-person account of Justice X's rescue into a job on a major metropolitan daily, and the loss of his virginity.

—You'd think that Kim Kozlowski would've come out of

this a hero, if anybody did—promotions, medals, the whole nine yards. And maybe she would have, if she hadn't told her boss to go shove Official Policy where the sun don't shine when he questioned her tactics. Last we heard, she was stuck back in mail fraud, and was considering an offer to teach High School civics in Minneapolis.

—As for us—while Jason's article minimized our role in the rescue of Justice X, (as compared to the role of, say, Jason Wolf), and while he didn't actually identify us by name, eager reporters soon came nosing after us like pigs after truffles.

Which is how come we had agreed to give an exclusive to Melissa Crane, just to get the rest of the pack off our backs, and to try to preserve some shred of our invisibility, not to mention our dignity. At least she was a serious scholar, we told ourselves, who we were fairly certain would never refer to us as the "Ragin' Agin" or the "gun totin' grannies" like certain members of the press corps.

And whatever her later betrayals, exaggerations, and downright falsehoods, at least she never did that.

Melissa Crane had asked to meet with me one last time before she sent her manuscript to the publisher.

"Just one little thing I wanted to run by you...," she said.

"Yes?"

"It's about—uh—the name of the book. See, with the kidnapping and Dr. Sloane and all, the marketing department feels this might have a certain mass appeal, but not with a title like "Post-Feminist Feminism and the New Millennium."

I could see her point.

"So they thought maybe 'Book Group from Hell', or—I love this one—'The Murderous Urges of Ordinary Women'. What do you think?"

What I thought was that I was beginning to get the picture. We'd been had. But maybe I'd known that all along, somewhere deep down.

"You never intended to write a scholarly work linking us to the line of women warriors going back to Queen Boadicea, did you?" I accused.

I should have been angry, I suppose, but in a way, I admired her devious, underhanded gumption. I saw a lot of myself in her, I guess, my younger self...

"I did. Honest I did," she hung her head, faking a remorse I was pretty sure she didn't feel. "But there weren't all that many of them—the women warriors—you know. And your story is so much more...readable...as a work of popular semi-fiction."

"Semi-fiction? You're going to turn us into a work of semi-fiction??"

"Truth-based semi-fiction," she looked up eagerly. "It's extremely hot right now."

Why didn't I stop her there and then? Threaten a lawsuit? Remind her she was dealing with people who'd already proven themselves capable of desperate acts?

I don't know. Yes, I'd grown fond of Melissa Crane. Yes, I hoped our story might inspire the next generation. But mostly, I didn't think there was much we could do. If we sued Melissa Crane for stealing our story, we'd have to admit we'd done all the things she claimed we'd done. And since the statute of limitations had not yet passed on some of those things, well…

It was over, anyway, the great adventure that had started that night at Cap'n Ahab's. We'd moved on to other things—Carole busy with her travels and her first grandchild; Ellie and Ramon working on "Decayed Beauty, the sequel"; Janet with her Shakespeare behind Bars project for women inmates; Mitch and I getting used to living together.

Or at least it was over for us.

But the idea of it had hit a chord.

And ideas can take on a life of their own.

Never doubt that a small group of thoughtful, committed citizens can change the world. Indeed, nothing else ever has.

From the message board at Calltoflabbyarms.com

Thanks so much sisters, for your contributions toward the purchase of a cow for the old women of Nambokha. Not only does she provide milk which can be sold at market for much-needed cash, but "Bessie" is also a rich source of manure for placing secretly in the beds of husbands who disturb the peace of the African night with their drunken foolishness.

I shall miss my beloved village, of course, and all the friends I've made, but my time as a volunteer in the Senior Peace Corps is drawing to a close. Yet it will be good to get back to the joys of refrigeration and indoor plumbing, and at least I will leave secure in the knowledge that I have helped in some small way to spread our "flabbyarms" message to this remote part of the globe.

You go girls!!

Sheila-Out-of-Africa

About the Author

Lois Meltzer is an attorney and a former humor columnist for a San Francisco newspaper. Her prize-winning work has appeared in *Seattle Weekly*, the *San Francisco Chronicle Magazine*, *Working Mother, Writer's Digest* and other publications. She also writes plays. Very funny plays. Her farce *Remain Seated* has been described as "what might happen if Lenny Bruce wrote screwball comedy."

Yet she remains an obscure, unjustly neglected writer. That she manages to keep a nice cheerful smile on her face (see photo), is a testament both to the resilience of the human spirit, and the benefits of excellent dental coverage.

She lives in the Pacific Northwest with a stuffed parrot named Waffles.

Made in the USA